Her hand fl[...] his face and connected hard against the side of his jaw

Time became a suspended entity, and her heart pumped a crazy agitated beat that sounded impossibly loud in the silence of the room.

"Does that make you feel better?" The sound of his voice resembled silk being razed by steel, and she forced her eyes to focus on his features.

"I have no intention of apologizing."

"I never imagined for one minute that you would," Jake drawled. His smile was a mere facsimile. "Any more than I intend to apologize for this."

Hard hands caught hold of her shoulders, and even as she struggled his arms imprisoned her close against him.

HELEN BIANCHIN, originally from New Zealand, met the man she would marry on a tobacco farm in Australia. Danilo, an Italian immigrant, spoke little English. Helen's Italian was nil. But communicate they did, and within eight weeks, Danilo found the words to ask Helen to marry him. With such romantic beginnings, it's a wonder that the author waited until after the birth of their third child to begin her prolific romance-writing career.

Books by Helen Bianchin

HARLEQUIN PRESENTS
975—DARK ENCHANTMENT
1111—AN AWAKENING DESIRE
1240—TOUCH THE FLAME
1383—THE TIGER'S LAIR
1423—THE STEFANOS MARRIAGE
1527—NO GENTLE SEDUCTION

HARLEQUIN ROMANCE
2010—BEWILDERED HAVEN
2084—AVENGING ANGEL
2175—THE HILLS OF HOME
2387—MASTER OF ULURU

HELEN BIANCHIN

Stormfire

Harlequin Books

TORONTO • NEW YORK • LONDON
AMSTERDAM • PARIS • SYDNEY • HAMBURG
STOCKHOLM • ATHENS • TOKYO • MILAN
MADRID • WARSAW • BUDAPEST • AUCKLAND

Harlequin Presents first edition June 1993
ISBN 0-373-11561-X

Original hardcover edition published in 1992
by Mills & Boon Limited

STORMFIRE

CHAPTER ONE

'LISETTE. Come on through.'

Rarely had Lisette heard Leith Andersen sound quite so affable. In his late fifties, the head partner of Andersen's was an austere, serious-minded man dedicated to the legal profession, approving strict formality to the degree that he was rarely known to use an employee's Christian name.

The fact that he had used *hers* made Lisette feel distinctly uncomfortable, and she proffered a polite smile as he rose to his feet and gestured towards one of three soft leather armchairs.

'Sit down, my dear.'

She took a seat with an elegant economy of movement, and was unable to still the kaleidoscopic sequence of possible eventualities that slipped through her brain. Perhaps she was to be made redundant? Yet that hardly made sense, for she handled an admirable amount of work, and the partner she liaised with was quite fulsome in praise with regard to her dedication to detail.

'Ah, I see you are perplexed.'

'Yes,' Lisette admitted frankly as he resumed his seat behind the large modern desk.

For some inexplicable reason she felt the beginnings of nervous tension, a strange prickling sensation that started in the pit of her stomach and gradually activated every single nerve in her body.

'I have been approached by an influential new client,' Leith Andersen relayed briskly. 'An exceedingly wealthy man whose entrepreneurial skills are well documented. He has vast holdings in America, Great Britain and Europe, and proposes to add to his existing investment portfolio within Australia.'

A feat which would generate an enormous amount of work, and a series of very fat legal fees for Andersen's, Lisette recognised silently.

'That's quite a coup,' she acknowledged with polite caution, unsure why she was being taken into the head partner's confidence.

'He has already leased a professional suite of offices, and is in the process of hiring suitable staff to complement his key personnel.' Leith paused fractionally, then spared her a kindly smile. 'I called you in to acquaint you of the facts, so that you would be prepared prior to meeting the client. I would like you to liaise with me on this.'

She attempted to school her features to mask her surprise. 'I am only a very junior member of the firm, Mr Andersen.'

'Nevertheless, you have earned a reputation for being extremely diligent.'

Such a compliment was rare, and she smiled cautiously in silent acceptance. 'May I ask where the client is presently based?'

'America, with branches in three major European capital cities.' He paused, casting her a long, speculative glance. 'I can assure you that his credentials are impeccable.'

'Of course,' Lisette accepted, aware of Leith Andersen's penchant for undertaking the most thorough investigation of any new client's credibility.

'His name——' He broke off at the sound of a discreet tap at the door. 'Ah, that will be him now.' Rising to his feet, he crossed the room as his secretary announced the client's arrival.

'Mr Hollingsworth.'

The blood drained from her face, leaving it waxen pale as she fought with rationale and won.

It couldn't be *Jake* Hollingsworth, surely? To her knowledge Jake hadn't set foot on Australian soil since his father's funeral. Besides, the chances that Leith Andersen's new client and Adam Hollingsworth's son might be one and the same man were incredibly remote.

Slowly she turned towards the door, her features schooled into a polite mask. Shock momentarily widened her hazel eyes, and all her fine body hairs rose up in protective self-defence as she became trapped by a disconcertingly direct steel-grey gaze.

For one totally mad moment she felt like a vulnerable small animal about to be devoured by a marauding jungle beast, and her chin lifted, tilting at a proud angle as she refused to break his gaze.

Jake Hollingsworth. Corporate raider, financial entrepreneur, and one of the most chillingly powerful men she had ever had the misfortune to meet.

In his late thirties, he appeared taller than she remembered, his broad-shouldered frame attired in an impeccably tailored dark grey business suit which did little to tame the raw virility he seemed able to project without any effort at all. Facial bone-structure portrayed a ruggedness that prevented him from being classically handsome, and its assemblage gave emphasis to a wide, sensuously moulded mouth and firm sculptured jaw.

Three years ago Jake Hollingsworth had been a formidable adversary, and one glance at his forbidding features was sufficient for Lisette to determine that nothing had changed.

'Please have a seat.'

Lisette was dimly aware of Leith Andersen's polite request followed by an equally smooth introduction, and she observed Jake's lurking cynicism as he affected an acknowledgement.

'Lisette.' His voice bore an American accent, and its drawling tone made a mockery of any veneer of politeness.

Leith Andersen's eyes sharpened, then assumed speculative interest. 'You know each other?'

'You could say that,' Jake acknowledged with undisguised cynicism. 'Lisette was married for a short time to my late father.'

There was a palpable silence for a few brief seconds, and Lisette unconsciously held her breath. Only a fool could have failed to detect the tensile steel beneath the calculated façade of politeness, or been aware of the degree of electric tension apparent.

'I have Lisette to thank for influencing your decision in favour of Andersen's?'

Jake's expression resembled an inscrutable mask, and his faint smile was a mere facsimile. 'My selection of your firm was based entirely on its reputation,' he declared with an inflexibility that made her flinch.

It was an evasion of the truth, or truth by deliberate omission, she decided hollowly. Jake Hollingsworth would never leave anything to chance, and she had little doubt that his selection of Andersen's was anything other than deliberate. The only unclear factor was his motive.

'Lisette's involvement should afford some loyalty to any vested interest the Hollingsworth empire validates within Australia,' Jake ventured smoothly. 'Unless, of course,' he continued silkily, 'Lisette would prefer to decline any personal participation?'

For an unguarded second her eyes blazed with anger, and her heart lurched painfully, then missed a beat.

Damn him, she cursed silently, longing to refuse. 'I know Adam would have wished me to offer you any assistance,' she conceded with the utmost politeness.

He inclined his head in silent acknowledgement, the expression in his eyes wholly cynical for a brief instant before he turned towards Leith Andersen. 'Shall we get down to business?'

For almost an hour she was forced to listen to Jake outlining concise details and eliciting pertinent facts from Leith Andersen. *Her* presence was a mere formality, and at no time was she required to comment or offer an opinion.

It was after six when Jake effected a conclusion to the consultation, and Lisette rose to her feet in silent gratitude, her nerves taut with tension as she preceded both men into the corridor.

Collecting her briefcase from her office, she walked quickly towards the lobby, aware too late of Jake's tall figure positioned indolently at ease adjacent to the trio of lifts.

A silent curse rose to the surface with the knowledge that she was equally doomed whether she retreated back into the office or crossed to stand at his side.

As if sensing her presence, he turned, and for a few timeless seconds her eyes seemed to lock with his, then she shifted her gaze to the lift doors as she silently willed one to arrive.

Jake made no attempt whatsoever at conversation, and she suffered his raking scrutiny with unblinking solemnity.

Consequently she was almost at screaming-point when the doors slid open to allow them entry, and only innate dignity permitted her to maintain an element of poise.

His presence was positively stifling, his powerful frame seeming to pose an unspoken threat in the close confines of the electronic cubicle, and she mentally derided herself for possessing too vivid an imagination.

How did you converse with a man whose very behaviour screamed his silent antipathy? Yet inherent good manners demanded she say *something*.

'Where are you staying?' The words came out with stilted formality, and she wondered a trifle wildly if she'd deliberately set herself up to be ignored. Except there was some solace in vindicating her conscience by making the first move.

It was crazy, but she was suddenly aware of her every visible feature: long, lustrous hair the colour of sable worn in a loose, upswept style, wide-spaced tawny hazel eyes, a generous, soft-curving mouth, and fine-textured pale skin. Conscious, also, that her petite stature made her look much younger than her twenty-five years.

Dark grey eyes speared hers, conveying a wealth of sardonic cynicism. 'Are you offering me a bed, Lisette?' he slanted with deliberate mockery. 'Or is this an attempt at polite conversation?'

Shock registered briefly before sheer rage rose to the surface, and for one utterly insane moment she considered hitting him. Her eyes blazed with an anger so intense that it was a wonder he didn't catch fire and burn, and a wealth of words rose damnably to the surface in vilification. Words she was entitled—*justified* to utter.

'You're Adam's son——'

'And we should be friends?' he intercepted in a deep mocking drawl.

In three years nothing had changed, and it infuriated her to see that he was silently awaiting her response.

She drew a deep breath, then slowly released it in an effort to retain some semblance of calm. 'I made that mistake once. I'm not foolish enough to repeat it.'

'*Foolish* is the last descriptive I'd accord you,' he alluded cynically, and she bit back a stinging retort.

She was *damned* if she'd resort to a slanging match. He had all the verbal tools at his command, and he'd never allow her to win.

'Why Australia, Jake? And why Melbourne in particular?'

'More pertinently—why Andersen's legal firm?' he countered with barely concealed mockery.

The lift came to a halt and the doors slid open. Without a word he gestured for her to precede him into the underground car park.

'I understood I had made my intention perfectly clear. The setting up of an Australian branch of Hollingsworth. A name I see you have chosen to discard.' He cast her a studied look that attempted to strip away the barriers protecting her soul, and his voice assumed hateful cynicism as he ventured, 'One can only wonder why.'

A spark of resentment lit her beautiful hazel eyes, and her chin lifted fractionally. During her brief marriage she had preferred to be known as Lisette LeClaire-Hollingsworth. Afterwards, she'd refused to utilise any influence Adam's name would have afforded.

'In the morning I'll inform Leith Andersen that working with you would amount to a conflict of interest,' she said stiffly.

His eyes never left hers, and she was conscious of every breath she took, every heartbeat, until she dragged her eyes away.

Three years ago she'd been shocked—*mesmerised*—by the dramatic aura of this man's animalistic sense of power. The passage of time, she discovered, had made little difference to her initial reaction to his primeval brand of sexual chemistry.

'If you do,' Jake revealed with dangerous softness, 'I'll ensure Leith Andersen is made aware that unless I can liaise with *you* I'll have no alternative but to seek the services of another legal firm.'

Dear lord in heaven, she agonised silently, *why*? Was he intent on some form of calculated revenge?

Yet it hardly seemed possible he'd wait two years after Adam's death to instigate it.

Her chin tilted fractionally, and her eyes were steady as she held his gaze. 'I fail to see what you can possibly gain from an invidious action that is clearly threatening and verges on blackmail.'

Jake smiled, a faint, mocking twist of his lips that held a wealth of cynicism. 'I could construe that to be a direct accusation. Perhaps you'd care to re-phrase?'

Anything she said would merely continue this war of words, and Lisette knew it was a battle she could never win. He was too formidable an opponent, and a dignified retreat was her only option.

Without a further word she turned and walked away from him. Inside, she was a mass of quivering nerves, her anger a volatile entity that threatened to erupt, and, quickening her step, she attempted to put as much distance as possible between them.

Reaching the bay where her car was parked, she unlocked the door, then slid in behind the wheel and fired the engine.

Damn him, she asserted with shaky anger as she engaged the gears and eased the BMW towards the exit. He was a force unto himself. Dangerously ruthless, and totally without mercy.

Lisette brought the car to a smooth halt as she fed her card into the automatic device, activating the barrier-arm release.

The flow of traffic leaving the city had diminished considerably, and she was grateful not to have to wait ages in long queues of cars that had little alternative but to crawl at a snail's pace through numerous computer-controlled intersections.

Despite her intention to banish Jake from her mind, it was impossible to stem a flood of memories that rose to the surface.

It had been during her final year at university that she'd met Adam Hollingsworth. By chance, he'd chosen to dine in the restaurant where she worked nights to supplement a meagre grant, and he soon became a frequent patron. An American, he was in Melbourne with the intention of extending his business interests, and at first she refused his invitations, citing work and study as a valid reason to decline. Although charming and friendly, it was clearly apparent he was considerably older than her own father, and she was hesitant, even given assurance that he merely wanted the pleasure of her company.

In an attempt to discourage him, she invited him to visit her home, intensely watchful of his reaction to the humble abode she shared with her French-born parents in one of the city's less salubrious suburbs. Despite the cleanliness apparent, their frugal existence couldn't be disguised, nor could the failing health of an invalid father or the proud demeanour of a mother who worked two jobs in an attempt to keep them financially afloat.

Adam persisted, and after a number of weeks Lisette relented, managing to convince herself that it wasn't 'dating'. On weekends he would drive her to any one of several scenic Reserves located on the outer reaches of the picturesque city for a picnic lunch, after which he'd insist she study while he relaxed with a book.

Intensely knowledgeable and genuinely caring, he proved to be someone who valued her friendship without making any sexual demands.

On his return to America he phoned every day, unperturbed at the cost of frequent long-distance calls, and jetted in to Melbourne every second week.

His proposal of marriage shocked her. Yet his reasons were clear and backed by medical proof. He had terminal cancer with only months, twelve at the most, left to live. Medication had rendered him impotent, making it impossible for him to consummate the relationship. Widowed several years previously, his only family comprised a son based in America, and he assured her that the marriage would merely be one of mutual convenience, from which she would gain financial assistance for herself and her parents. In return he sought only the right to claim her companionship for what must inevitably be the last year of his life.

Her father had been too ill to do more than voice a token protest, and one look at her mother's strained features—the spark of hope that momentarily lit those tired eyes—was sufficient for Lisette to accept.

Adam's son was an entirely different matter. He flew over from the States for his father's wedding, and one glance at his formidably ruthless features was sufficient for Lisette to realise Jake could never be anything other than an enemy.

Granted, he was civil, even distantly polite. But only a fool could have doubted that he had categorised his father's second wife as a gold-digging opportunist, and branded his father a gullible fool.

Adam kept his word, immediately setting wheels in motion to relinquish the reins of business to Jake with the excuse that he was opting for an early retirement in order to spend more time with his young wife. He allocated sufficient funds to ensure her father was adequately cared for, therefore enabling her mother to be free of any financial burden. He bought an apartment in the exclusive suburb of Toorak, and insisted that Lisette complete her law degree.

Together they enjoyed a relaxed, informal lifestyle. Adam became her best friend, confidant, ally—her salvation when her father died mere months after her marriage.

Her graduation ceremony proved to be a bittersweet occasion, for, although Adam insisted on attending, it became obvious his strength was rapidly failing, and one night he simply went to sleep and never awoke.

Lisette retained very little memory of those ensuing few weeks. Her sadness at losing Adam was overshadowed by the presence of his son demanding answers to questions which she felt helpless to give any conclusive response to. It hadn't been her decision to leave Jake totally unaware of the extent of his father's illness, and Jake's barely held wrath was a palpable entity from which she'd shakily withdrawn.

Dismayed to learn Adam had bequested her half his personal fortune, she instructed his solicitors to inform Jake's American advisers that she was contesting the will, retaining only the apartment, the BMW, and sufficient selected investments Adam had gifted her during their brief marriage to ensure her financial security. Deeds assigning legal ownership to Jake of various real estate holdings in Australia were prepared on her instructions, and signed.

There had been no direct contact, merely an expressed acknowledgement via Jake's legal representatives for the hefty bequest she had declined in his favour.

As far as Jake Hollingsworth was concerned, it was almost as if she had ceased to exist, Lisette reflected pensively as she garaged the car beneath the exclusive block of apartments.

Her apartment was situated on the seventh floor, and the peal of the phone greeted her as she unlocked the door. For a few totally mad seconds she froze as sheer nervous tension manifested itself in a painful knot in the region of her stomach.

Then common sense prevailed. Her number was ex-directory, she consoled at once, angry with herself for even imagining that Jake Hollingsworth's power could possibly extend to the disclosure of her private set of coded digits. And even if he chose to wield such influence, *why* would he resort to phoning her when he could derive so much more satisfaction from visually witnessing her discomfort at the office?

Crossing the lobby, she picked up the receiver and uttered her customary greeting.

'Maman,' Lisette breathed with shaky relief, lapsing at once into their customary French. It was a habit they adopted whenever they were together, affording mother and daughter the opportunity to maintain fluency in their native language. 'How are you?'

'More to the point, *chérie*—how are you? Were you not expecting my call?'

'Of course,' she assured at once. 'I had to stay late at the office, and only this minute arrived home.'

'So—how was your day?' Louise LeClaire queried, and Lisette had a clear picture of her mother seated on the comfortable sofa in the lounge of her elegantly furnished suburban home in Frankston overlooking Port Phillip Bay.

She wanted to say, Adam's son is in Melbourne, and I don't understand why. Instead, she remained silent.

Maman would immediately put into words all Lisette's own fears and insecurities and, while they persisted, she wasn't ready to confront them just yet.

Instead, she relayed an interesting discourse of events that had taken place that day—amusing anecdotes she knew her mother would enjoy. Fifteen minutes—sometimes twenty—then they would each bid the other goodnight.

Their shared closeness was more attuned to friends than mother and daughter, and Lisette frequently escaped the city at weekends for the relative peace and tranquillity of her mother's home.

Wait, a tiny voice cautioned. Maybe you're wrong, Jake Hollingsworth's presence in Australia, and particularly Melbourne, could be legitimate.

Yet Lisette found it impossible not to feel tense and on edge, rather like the victim of a predatory animal, unsure where and when the assault would take place and whether it would be for the kill or merely the satisfaction of the chase.

CHAPTER TWO

THE following afternoon Lisette picked up her extension to find Jake on the other end of the line.

'I'll be in Sydney for the next few days.' His voice was a deep, faintly accented drawl and totally devoid of any conventional preamble. 'One of my associates will liaise with you during my absence. Can you see him this afternoon?'

Calmly, efficiently, she re-scheduled appointments to allow the priority Leith Andersen had insisted Jake Hollingsworth be accorded. 'Threethirty? His name?'

'Hank Preston.'

'I'll look forward to meeting him,' she responded with stilted politeness, and replaced the receiver before he had the opportunity to add anything further.

Score one for Lisette LeClaire, who could be just as concise as Adam's son. Although she was aware any victory over Jake would be fleeting.

Hank Preston entered her office at the appointed time, a tall, lean Texan possessed of undoubted charm and shrewd business acumen. He also asked her out to dinner—an offer she politely declined on the grounds that she was already committed to sharing an evening meal with her mother.

'Tomorrow night,' Hank insisted, shooting her a sloping smile as he sensed her reluctance. 'Business, if that's the way you want it.' As if to

convince her, he added, 'I'll be out all day in-
specting property. There'll be a sheaf of paperwork
for you to peruse, prior to arranging a search of
the relevant title deeds.' His features took on a
watchful expression. 'Jake only hires those who
dedicate one hundred per cent of their time, with
a bonus added in return for conscientious effort.'

Lisette set down her pen, and surveyed the man
in front of her with care. 'And if I refuse, will I be
responsible for putting your bonus for this particular job in jeopardy?'

'Not at all,' he declared smoothly.

Yet if she declined, he would report back to Jake,
who in turn would acquaint Leith Andersen of her
lack of co-operation, and she had no particular
desire to blot her copybook with Leith Andersen
and restrict her advancement within the firm. 'Very
well, then.' Decisiveness had to be an advantage.
'What time, and where?'

Hank Preston named an inner-city hotel, and she
agreed to meet him at seven the following evening.

The remainder of the day proved relatively uneventful, and the cares of the past twenty-four hours
seemed to lift considerably as she edged the BMW
on to the Nepean Highway and covered the ensuing
kilometres to Frankston, where, after a perfect
meal, she relaxed and pushed Jake Hollingsworth
to the furthest edge of her mind.

'You look—preoccupied, *chérie*,' Louise ventured as they took their coffee in the lounge, and
Lisette summoned forth a faintly rueful smile.

'Maybe because I am,' she owned, aware of her
mother's acute perceptiveness.

'A client, perhaps, who ruffles your feathers more than a little?'

That had to be the understatement of the year! 'You could say that.'

'This man, who is he?'

'So positive it is a man, Maman?'

Louise effected a light shrugging gesture. 'Of course,' she teased. 'I am very pleased for you.'

Lisette shook her head in despair. 'I don't even like him.' *Like* was too tame a descriptive for someone of Jake Hollingsworth's dynamic calibre!

'*Naturellement*,' her mother responded with dry humour. 'One never does, at first.' A faint smile tugged the edges of her mouth. 'I shall be most interested to observe what transpires.'

Lisette cast her mother a wry glance. 'It will be a wasted exercise.'

'We shall see.'

It was late when they retired for the night, and in the morning Lisette rose early, ate a light breakfast, then drove into the city.

For the remainder of the day she worked at a fairly hectic pace, enjoying the challenge presented in coping with several appointments and the resultant paperwork. Lunch was a hastily eaten sandwich and two cups of coffee, and she didn't leave the office until well after five.

There was time for a leisurely shower and a quick snack before preparing for her dinner engagement with Hank Preston.

Opting to present a professional image, Lisette selected a slim-fitting tailored suit in fine-checked black and white wool. Black accessories completed the outfit, and she used minimum make-up with emphasis on her eyes. Her hair was coaxed into a chignon worn at her nape, and she slung a woollen coat over her shoulders to ward off the cold mid-winter temperatures.

The air was heavy with the threat of rain, and huge splashes began to batter her windscreen within minutes of leaving Toorak. By the time she reached the city it had assumed the proportions of a deluge.

Parking was achieved with minimal effort, for she simply drove to the hotel entrance and handed her keys to the attendant for valet parking.

The restaurant was situated on the first floor, and she entered the lobby a few minutes after seven to find Hank enjoying a drink at the adjoining bar.

'How nice,' he drawled in appreciation as he moved forward to greet her. 'A punctual female.' His smile was pleasantly warm. 'What will you have to drink?'

She would have loved a brandy to take the chill out of her bones, but anything alcoholic on an empty stomach was guaranteed to go straight to her head.

'Mineral water will be fine,' Lisette told him as he saw her seated in a comfortable chair.

Ten minutes later the *maître d'* escorted them to their table.

Lisette ordered soup and followed it with veal scallopini and assorted vegetables, declined dessert in favour of the cheeseboard, and acceded to Hank's suggestion that he order a bottle of wine.

Conversation was confined to business, and she had just begun on the main course when Hank paused mid-sentence to observe, 'Jake is back from Sydney earlier than expected, and has obviously chosen to act on a recommendation we both received for this particular restaurant.'

The possibility that their presence might go undetected was unlikely, and she felt the nerves in her stomach clench in sheer reaction at the prospect of a confrontation.

She turned slightly, and her eyes met his with steady regard, unblinking and resolute as she inclined her head.

'Lisette. Hank,' Jake acknowledged. His voice was deep and deceptively polite, yet for some reason it made all her fine body hairs stand up on end in reactionary self-defence.

For an instant his eyes slid over the tailored cut of her jacket before slowly travelling up to rest on her scarlet-lipsticked mouth.

Implacable, emotionless, and totally lacking in humility, she perceived, aware that, although his features were assembled into a polite mask, the depths of his eyes were dark and unfathomable.

Lisette's gaze slid to the stunning blonde at his side, noting her height and curvaceous figure in one sweeping glance.

'Enjoy your meal,' Jake bade silkily as he directed his companion towards a table a short distance away.

He obviously chose not to mix business with pleasure, Lisette decided a trifle churlishly. One look at his glamorous companion was sufficient to determine that business was the last thing on his mind.

Attired in an impeccably tailored dark suit, white linen shirt and sombre tie, he looked every inch the powerful potentate, presenting a striking mesh of sensual sexuality and compelling authority that gained the attention of every female in the room.

Except hers, Lisette acknowledged silently as she concentrated on doing her meal the justice it deserved.

Quite deliberately she engaged Hank in conversation, trading on his easygoing nature to elicit information that was mainly inconsequential.

'Seven years,' Hank responded in answer to her query regarding the length of time he'd spent in Hollingsworth International's employ. 'And no, I don't have a wife waiting patiently back home,' he added with a sloping smile. 'Jake believes in the family unit. If a married staff member is required to travel, the wife and family gets to go along. Company policy.' His smile widened. 'The marital status of a prospective employee is of prime importance for the particular position he has in mind.'

'How noble.'

Her facetiousness drew a raised eyebrow. 'I thought today's women were deeply into equality of the sexes and role-sharing.'

'I'm sure they are.'

'But you're not?'

'I didn't say that,' Lisette said carefully, aware she'd inadvertently aroused his interest. 'Would you mind if we leave after we've had our coffee? I have a heavy day ahead of me, and I——'

'Need your beauty sleep?' He pushed his plate aside and signalled for the waiter. 'And here I was hoping to persuade you to show me at least one of the city's favoured nightspots.'

It was ages since she'd gone out on a date. *Years.* Certainly before she met Adam, and then only as one in a group of university students. Her natural reserve made her cautious, even wary. A serene, tranquil existence seemed infinitely preferable to succumbing to passions of the flesh.

'Thank you, but no,' she said with apparent regret, and he indicated quietly,

'I had hoped the ring you wear was little more than a fashion accessory. But I see that I'm wrong.'

'The man who put it there meant a great deal to me.'

His eyes sharpened fractionally. '*Meant?*'

She looked at him steadily for a few seconds. 'My husband,' she explained simply. 'He died two years ago.'

'You can't envisage anyone taking his place—ever?'

The query was gently voiced, and she merely smiled. 'Shall we leave?'

Lisette wondered how Hank would react if she were to reveal that her late husband was Jake's father. A fact which made her Hank's revered boss's *stepmother*.

Dear lord, what a contradiction in terms, she concluded silently, aware that Hank was obviously in ignorance of her true identity, and a tiny flame of resentment flared that she might in any way be regarded by Jake as a hypothetical skeleton in his family closet.

Hank signed the bill, pocketed the slip, then placed a hand at Lisette's elbow to escort her from the restaurant.

'Did you come by cab?'

Lisette indicated the stairs leading down to the lobby.

'I drove my car. The concierge has the key.'

It had been a pleasant evening, and she said as much as the BMW swept to a halt outside the main entrance.

'I'll be in touch,' Hank declared warmly, and she smiled as she slid in behind the wheel and engaged the gears.

It was almost ten when she arrived at her apartment, and, feeling oddly restless, she discarded her clothes, donned nightwear and slipped her arms into a warm robe before entering the kitchen.

A glass of hot milk laced with brandy should soothe her fractured nerves and help her sleep, she determined as she set about the task with automatic movements, and when the milk was ready she carried it through to the lounge.

Jake Hollingsworth's image rose up to taunt her, his compelling features so startlingly vivid that she had to blink several times to dispel them.

In the restaurant she had been supremely conscious of his presence. A fact she found disturbing, to say the least. She couldn't help wondering if Jake had deliberately chosen the same restaurant, knowing Hank had already booked a table there.

A hollow laugh rose and died in her throat, and her fingers tightened around the handle of her cup. Now she was being paranoid!

Impossibly angry with herself, she activated the remote control to switch on the television, deliberately summoning interest in a thirty-minute documentary until it finished.

Sleep was never more distant, and with detached resolve she crossed to her briefcase, withdrew a ribboned folder of collected papers and settled down to study them.

It was after one when, weary with mental exhaustion, she replaced the folder and went to bed.

'Lisette. Mr Andersen would like to see you in his office.'

Lisette stifled a silent groan. It was ten minutes prior to her accustomed lunch-break, and she desperately needed at least one strong cup of coffee and something to eat. She'd been so tired last night that she'd forgotten to set the alarm, had overslept, and hadn't paused for even the quickest snack before dashing into the city.

'I'm on my way.'

She took care to check her lipstick before moving towards the large front office, and she summoned a pleasant smile as the head partner's secretary tapped on the door before announcing her presence.

Leith Andersen was seated at his desk. Opposite him, looking every inch the corporate warlord and portraying controlled ease, was Jake Hollingsworth.

Both men rose to their feet, one silent and intently watchful, the other beaming and faintly effusive as he indicated one of two adjacent chairs.

'Sit down, Lisette,' Leith Andersen bade genially. 'Mr Hollingsworth would like a progress report.'

Would he, indeed! 'I gave Hank Preston all the relevant paperwork last night,' she forced herself to relay carefully. She glanced towards Jake, and immediately wished she hadn't, for his gaze held an unwavering, faintly cynical quality which was positively nerve-racking. 'I have copies in my office.'

'Perhaps we could discuss it over lunch,' Jake invited smoothly, and at once she felt trapped.

'What an excellent suggestion,' Leith Andersen agreed, looking at Lisette for her spoken acceptance.

'I'm sorry,' she refused politely. 'I already have a luncheon engagement.' It took considerable courage to appear apologetic, and she even managed a slight smile in apparent regret. 'I can, however,' she offered sweetly, 're-shuffle my appointments this afternoon and fit you in around three.'

Jake's eyes darkened infinitesimally. 'This afternoon is out. We'll have to make it dinner.'

Lunch would have been the lesser of the two evils, for at least then she could have insisted on a maximum hour. Dinner would involve two hours at least.

She stifled a silent curse as she met his gaze, aware from the slightly mocking glint that he had anticipated her initial refusal and deliberately sought to place her at a disadvantage.

'If you insist,' Lisette acceded politely.

'Seven,' he told her. 'I'll collect you.'

'Name the restaurant, and I'll meet you there.' The words were proffered sweetly, but there was nothing sweet about the determined glance she cast him.

One eyebrow rose fractionally, and the corner of his mouth lifted with cynical humour. 'I appreciate your preference for independence, but in this instance you're going to have to indulge me.' His gaze was direct, openly daring her to thwart him. 'Besides,' he added with chilling softness, 'my father would turn in his grave if I failed to take adequate care of you.'

I don't need taking care of, she longed to fling at him. Especially by *you*. In Leith Andersen's hearing there was only one thing she could say, and she managed it with an outward display of graciousness. 'Thank you.'

There would be time enough when they were alone to upbraid him. In fact, it would give her infinite pleasure!

His eyes assumed a cynical gleam. Almost as if he perceived the threat of her intent, and was amused at the prospect of a confrontation. Damn him. What she wouldn't give to physically *hit* him! If he continued with this line of attack, maybe she *would*, she resolved silently.

With considerable poise she rose to her feet, then took her leave.

It was just as well she had a hectic afternoon ahead of her, and for the next few hours she dealt with a pile of paperwork, made necessary phone calls, and left the city after five-thirty to battle her way through a maze of slow-moving traffic that began to ease only slightly as she drew close to her apartment.

Her temper wasn't aided by the discovery that she'd neglected to include some important notes in her briefcase prior to leaving the office, and she crossed to the phone with the intention of cancelling the evening, only to come to an abrupt halt with the realisation that she had no idea where Jake Hollingsworth was staying.

Damn. Now she'd have to go. Unless she waited until he arrived, then told him of her change of mind. Except she wouldn't put it past him to calmly negate every excuse she offered and insist on conducting their meeting *here*. Given an alternative, she'd opt for a restaurant. At least then she could walk out on him at will and summon a taxi home.

Choosing something suitable to wear posed doubt in her mind, and she mentally reviewed her wardrobe as she took a quick shower and washed her hair. Anything *too* conservative would elicit his amusement, yet if she selected something remotely frivolous...

Lisette worked conditioner into her hair, then stood beneath the jet of water for as long as she dared before drying off and completing her toilette.

At five to seven she was ready, secure in the knowledge that the beaded V-necked scarlet evening jumper she'd chosen to wear with a black tailored skirt was sufficiently elegant. Black high-heeled shoes completed the outfit. She had deliberately left her make-up understated, and opted to wear her hair in a casual upswept style. Her mirrored image reflected poise and undoubted *élan*, and one glance at her pensive expression was sufficient to persuade her mouth into a slight smile.

At precisely seven there was a knock on her door, and a puzzled frown momentarily creased her brow as she crossed the room.

The apartment block possessed the ultimate in hi-tech security, and only the outer door of the main entrance lobby downstairs opened automatically. A surveillance camera monitored the lobby area and reception, and every apartment had audio-visual intercom.

As a precaution she checked the spyhole, and disbelief clouded her eyes as Jake Hollingsworth's forceful features came into view.

Releasing the lock, she opened the door. 'How did you get into the building?'

He appeared vaguely satanical in a dark grey coat worn over an equally dark suit, and for some reason the nerves inside her stomach completed an unexpected flip before settling into a painful knot.

He really was *too* much, she decided as she managed a polite greeting. Too tall—at least for her diminutive height. And his shoulders were too broad. In comparison she felt ridiculously petite, and *young*. She could have added—gauche. It wasn't a feeling she enjoyed.

'Adam bought two apartments in this apartment block,' he revealed drily. 'One he gifted you, and the other I chose to retain. It makes an ideal base while I'm in Melbourne.'

Which explained why he had been able to circumvent the usual security measures. A coil of anger tightened painfully in Lisette's chest at the thought of having him stay within such close proximity.

'Two floors above you,' Jake informed her, almost as if he could read her mind. 'In an identical location.' His eyes gleamed as they roved her expressive features. 'Are you going to ask me in, or shall we leave?'

To have him intrude into her space was something she'd prefer to avoid. 'Leave,' she indicated without hesitation, and without a further word she collected her coat and evening-purse.

His car was a Jaguar, and seated inside its leather-cushioned, heated interior she couldn't help likening Jake to the jungle beast represented by the vehicle's design.

'Shall we attempt neutrality via polite conversation?'

His drawled query merely served to tighten the nerves inside her stomach, and she proffered a slight smile as she turned towards him. 'Silence might be safer.'

'Not, one hopes, for the entire evening?'

Her fingers clenched into her palms, their tapered manicured length digging painfully into the soft flesh as she fought to restrain her anger. 'It might amuse you to assert superiority during working hours, but outside the office we're on equal terms.'

'A warning, Lisette?' he slanted with damning cynicism.

'A statement.'

The restaurant Jake had chosen was intimately small, tastefully furnished, and exclusive.

'Iced water,' she requested when asked her preference, and to her surprise Jake nodded and ordered the same for himself.

He sat well back in his chair, his expression enigmatic as he subjected her to a deliberate appraisal. It was maddening to feel akin to a butterfly pinned to the wall, but the sensation was impossible to repress. Often the best form of defence was attack, and she forced herself to return his gaze with unblinking solemnity.

'Shall I give you a verbal run-down now?' she queried with outward calm. 'I've brought a copy of my notes for easy reference.'

'If there was any urgency, I would have had you fax the information through to me.'

A chill feathered its way down the length of her spine at his drawled response, and resentment flared. 'In that case, why am I here?'

The edges of his mouth twisted to form a faintly sardonic smile. 'You couldn't make lunch, so I suggested dinner.'

Any response she might have made was put on hold out of deference to the waiter, who presented them each with a menu, proffered his suggestions, then left them to make their selection.

Her appetite seemed to have fled, and she said as much, opting for the *soupe du jour*.

'No main course?'

'No.'

'I refuse to believe you have a need to diet. Why not try the fish?' Jake queried mildly.

There was nothing remotely mild about the dark, piercing glance he directed at her, and she deliberately schooled her features into a polite mask.

'I'm not hungry.'

'Surely we can share a meal together?' He was deliberately baiting her in an attempt to break through the barrier of her control, and it irked unbearably.

'So that you can play cat to my mouse?'

His expression was an inscrutable shield, without so much as a flicker of emotion visible on those broad sculptured features.

'Is that what you think?'

Lisette fought with politeness and lost. 'Forgive me, but I don't feel inclined to enter into a verbal fencing match.' She stood to her feet and gathered up her coat and bag.

'Sit down.' His voice was cool, inflexible, and she felt the sheer force of his will as she met the implacability evident in those dark eyes.

'I should never have come.' The words slipped unheeded from her lips as she stood poised for flight, and her eyes widened as his fingers closed over her wrist.

'Yet you did,' Jake reminded her quietly.

'You gave me little choice.'

'Perhaps not.'

She tried to free her hand, and failed. 'Let me go, damn you!' It was an impassioned plea from the heart, and reflected a mixture of anger and outrage.

'Why not sit down and order?' he suggested imperturbably.

'I'm not into *pretence*. Nor do I appreciate any heavy-handed macho tactics.' Her eyes were dark golden-green crystalline shards. 'If you don't let me go, I'll cause a scene.'

For a moment she thought he meant to insist, and her eyes warred openly with his, hostile with the threat of her intent.

'It won't do any good to run away.'

'I am not running away,' she spat with measured fury. 'I simply can't bear to spend another minute in your company!' She was past caring that her actions were causing circumspect attention from fellow patrons.

'I'll have the waiter order you a cab.'

Without a word he released her hand, and she immediately turned and wove her way between tables to the foyer, inclined her head to the startled *maître d'*, then swept out through the door.

The cold blast of winter air hit her face, and she slid into her coat. The drizzle that had prevailed through most of the day had now turned into sweeping rain, and she cursed her foolishness in walking out before a taxi could arrive.

Yet even as she glanced along the pavement, she sighted a cruising taxi and hurriedly hailed it, breathing a sigh of relief when the driver pulled into the kerb. At that moment Jake emerged from the restaurant, and beneath the reflected neon lighting his features resembled a ruthless mask.

Lisette shivered slightly against the apprehensive curl of nervous tension inside her stomach as he began walking towards the taxi.

'Is he with you, lady?'

The sound of the driver's voice galvanised her into action, and she quickly slipped into the back seat and closed the door. 'No. Toorak,' she instructed, giving him the street location.

Ten minutes later she was safely inside her apartment, slightly shaken, but immensely thankful to be free from Jake's forceful presence.

CHAPTER THREE

LISETTE slept badly, and woke with a feeling of foreboding that haunted her for most of the day, intruding to such an extent that the nerves in her stomach clenched every time her desk phone rang.

It was impossible to imagine that Jake would allow any woman to walk out on him. With his undoubted physical attraction and wealth, it was unlikely any female had ever displayed such folly, she decided shakily as she collected a sheaf of photocopies and placed them into her briefcase prior to leaving the office.

Even the weather seemed to conspire against her, with wind-driven rain lashing against the windscreen, bitterly cold temperatures, and the added frustration of being caught in stop-start traffic as a heavier than usual flow of vehicles attempted to vacate the city.

It was a relief to enter her apartment, and she activated the heating control panel, then crossed to the bedroom to change her formal office wear for something infinitely more comfortable.

Her evening meal comprised a large bowl of home-made chicken and vegetable soup, followed by fresh fruit, and when the dishes were dispensed into the dishwasher she sat down at the escritoire to work on her notes.

The sharp staccato knock sounded loud in the silence of the room, and Lisette frowned, then cast her watch a quick glance as she crossed the room to the front door.

Jake's features immediately came into view through the spyhole, and her pulse-rate immediately went into overdrive.

Disregarding her initial instinct, she opened the door, then stood in questioning silence as he loomed incredibly large in the aperture. He exuded an elemental ruthlessness beneath his sophisticated façade, so that it was impossible to discern whether he was here in the guise of friend or foe.

'Aren't you going to ask me in?'

She hesitated, then said stiffly, 'I have a sheaf of paperwork to get through.'

'As it's *my* paperwork, I absolve you from working on it tonight,' he drawled, and a faint shiver slithered its way down the length of her spine.

Resentment flared briefly as she met his steady gaze, and she glimpsed the cool, assessing quality apparent there, the strangely watchful element that made her feel like the vulnerable prey of a jungle predator.

'I'm responsible to Leith Andersen.'

'Who in turn takes instruction from me.'

She drew in her breath and slowly released it. 'I can give you half an hour.'

'How generous.'

For one crazy moment she wished she hadn't changed out of her office clothes. Attired in a comfortable tracksuit, no make-up, and her hair caught together in a single braid, she looked like a schoolgirl.

The only way she could handle his presence was to pretend polite indifference, and she indicated the lounge with a sweep of her hand.

He moved past her, and she felt positively dwarfed without the benefit of high heels. The lounge suddenly seemed much smaller, and she indicated a sofa. 'Please sit down.'

The request was little more than a formality, and he turned slightly to regard her with mocking indulgence.

'So polite, Lisette?'

'How would you have me behave?'

The edges of his mouth curved fractionally higher, and for a moment his eyes speared hers with merciless disregard before he turned away to glance around the room.

'This is almost exactly as I remember it.'

'Adam had excellent taste,' Lisette commended quietly.

'He bought this apartment and furnished it to please *you*.'

She forced herself to meet his eyes. 'Adam merely enquired if I held any particular dislike with regard to interior décor. I chose the colour scheme, that's all.'

'And elected to stay here after his death.'

'Why should I move?' she ventured steadily. It took every ounce of resolve to stand there with apparent calm when inside her nerves were fracturing into a thousand splinters.

'Why, indeed?' His voice was a velvet drawl, and she forced herself to query,

'I presume you have a reason for coming here?'

'Need I remind you we have my father in common?' he asked silkily.

A lump rose in her throat, which she nervously attempted to swallow. 'During the past three years you've chosen to ignore my existence.'

'Accepting someone twelve years my junior in any *maternal* image was impossible.'

She forced herself to hold his gaze. 'You made that abundantly clear at the time.'

'What did you expect, Lisette? Familial affection? Surely you can't be that naïve?'

The desire to retaliate was almost impossible to resist, and she clenched her hands in an attempt at control. He was deliberately baiting her, searching for any visible chink in her armour.

'You're a fascinating enigma,' he declared in a voice that was silky and infinitely dangerous. 'A woman-child, with an air of innocence that has to be contrived.' His eyes slid slowly down to her breasts in deliberate appraisal and lingered there over-long before slipping down to her waist and slender hips, then he began an upward trail to halt at her mouth. He smiled, a slight hint of self-mockery parting his lips as he revealed even white teeth. 'Yet no *child* could have successfully trapped a man three times her age into providing a wedding-ring, and gifting her a fortune.' He thrust hands into his trouser pockets, and regarded her in silence for several seconds.

If he hoped to unnerve her, she didn't allow him any visual sign of succeeding, and after what seemed an age he taunted softly, 'Was it worth it, Lisette?'

Knowing just how much pleasure Adam had derived from her companionship, she didn't hesitate. 'Yes.'

'You could have set yourself up for life, and never had to work again. Why didn't you?'

He wanted to annihilate her—she could see it in his eyes, the silent threat evidenced in his stance, and the mercury determining the level of her anger rose several points.

'Adam gifted me the apartment when he bought it. As well as the car, and a portfolio of selected investments he insisted bear my name.' She held his gaze with innate dignity. 'More than enough to adequately ensure I need never worry about keeping the figurative wolf from my door.'

'Yet those assets were a mere pittance in comparison to the total sum of my father's wealth,' Jake pursued with dangerous softness.

'I had no knowledge of Adam's financial affairs,' she denied at once. 'And any assets other than those he gifted me during his lifetime were rightfully yours.'

His gaze hardened until the depths of his eyes resembled polished onyx, and a flare of resentment began to flame deep inside, fuelling her anger.

'Why did you come here?' she demanded.

His gaze speared hers, hard and incredibly merciless. 'To talk.' He paused slightly, then continued in a dangerously silky voice, 'Surely that is permissible?'

'*Why*?' She seemed to have lost any pretence at good manners, and it angered her unbearably that this man could reduce her to such an unenviable state.

'In the office you insist on maintaining a businesslike image. Last night you walked out on what was meant to be a social occasion.'

'I fail to see the need for any social contact between us,' she said stiffly, and hated the sardonic cynicism evident on his strongly etched features.

'No? It would be impolite of me to ignore you while I'm in Melbourne. Besides, I have a compelling desire to discover precisely what fascination you held for my father,' he informed her with hateful cynicism. 'To such an extent that he would consider leaving you the bulk of his personal fortune.'

'Aren't you forgetting that I refused almost *all* that fortune?' she threw angrily, her eyes clashing openly with his own. Helpless rage filled her, erupting into cold, angry speech as she walked towards the foyer. 'I'd like you to leave.'

'Not yet.'

'If you don't,' she insisted, almost shaking with fury, 'I'll call security and inform them you're an unwelcome guest.'

His eyes were hard and obdurate, reflecting an inflexible strength of will that feathered fear down the length of her spine. 'If you do, be aware I'll present credentials and inform them you've overreacted in a minor domestic dispute.' His voice assumed an icy intensity. 'However, be warned I fully intend our working relationship to continue for as long as it pleases me.' His smile was totally without humour, and he looked at her for what seemed an age in a deliberate attempt at silent intimidation. 'And should you rashly consider resigning from the company, you might do well to remember I wield considerable power.'

The blood chilled in her veins, and for a moment shocked disbelief vied with outrage. 'I won't permit you to threaten me!'

'You must be aware,' he continued softly, 'just how necessary it is for a member of the legal fraternity to maintain an unimpeachable profile.'

'There is nothing you could do or say that would damage my reputation.'

His eyes assumed sardonic cynicism. 'The gossipmongers will have a field day if rumour relays that after successfully pursuing my father you have now transferred your attention to his son.'

Innuendo, carefully orchestrated and embellished, could spread like wildfire, and prove immensely distressing both privately and professionally.

Lisette would have given anything to have ruffled that imperturbable composure, and her eyes sparked hateful fire. 'Do that, and I'll sue you for slander.'

'Aren't you forgetting the evidence is already very much against you?'

Without thought her hand flashed towards his face and connected hard against the side of his jaw.

The enormity of her action was reflected in her eyes. Never before had she experienced such anger, and not once had she ever lifted a hand against anyone.

Time became a suspended entity, and her heart pumped a crazy agitated beat that sounded impossibly loud in the silence of the room.

'Does that make you feel better?' The sound of his voice resembled silk being razed by steel, and she forced her eyes to focus on his features.

The air between them seemed charged with electric tension, and she was held mesmerised by the darkness of his eyes, the threat of something she didn't dare attempt to define.

'I have no intention of apologising.' Was that her voice? It sounded low and husky with suppressed anger.

'I never imagined for one minute that you would,' Jake drawled. His smile was a mere facsimile. 'Any more than I intend to apologise for *this*.'

Hard hands caught hold of her shoulders, and even as she struggled his arms imprisoned her close against him.

There was no power on earth that could prevent the slow downward descent of his head, or the un-erring possession of his mouth as it closed over hers in a plundering invasion that violated her very soul.

It was an onslaught aimed specifically at sub-jugation, and when he finally released her she could only look at him, her eyes mirroring an accusatory mixture of shock and humiliation.

Her lips felt numb and swollen, the inner tissues grazed where they had been heartlessly ground against her teeth, and her throat ached with sup-pressed emotion.

Firm fingers caught hold of her chin, and her lashes swiftly lowered in automatic self-defence against the threat of angry tears.

Uncaring, she struck at his hand, then cried out as he caught both her wrists and held them in a merciless grip. Immediately she wrenched at them with fruitless impatient movements that merely served to increase her anger.

'Let me go, damn you!'

His gaze was frighteningly dark, even threatening, and she wondered at her own temerity in defying him.

'You egotistical, tyrannical *bastard*! Who do you think you are?'

His smile was without humour, and for the first time she experienced real fear. Suddenly she realised just how vulnerable her position was, alone and terribly outclassed when it came to matching his physical strength.

He regarded her in silence, his eyes partly hooded beneath heavy lids, making it impossible to read his expression.

'Consider we're even,' Jake drawled. He lifted a hand and brushed his fingers against her lips, feeling their trembling softness an instant before she turned her head away.

'Get out!'

His fingers slid to the edge of her jaw, tilting it fractionally as he forced her to meet his gaze for a few timeless seconds before he lowered his head to recapture her mouth.

Expecting further retribution, Lisette was totally unprepared for the firm, coaxing quality of his lips or the persuasive probing of his tongue, and her startled gasp of protest was lost as he began an evocative, sensual exploration that threatened to totally overwhelm her.

Of its own volition, her heart tripped and began a rapid erratic beat, and, while one part of her registered recognition of an explosive sexual chemistry, the other screamed in silent vilification.

Each separate nerve-ending assumed an acute sensitivity, heightening her sensual awareness to a degree that made her feel exhilaratingly alive for a few heart-stopping seconds before fear cooled the rapidly pulsing blood in her veins and left her feeling terribly afraid. A silent moan of entreaty rose in her throat, and she wrenched her mouth away from his, using both hands to push against his chest in an effort to be free of him.

The fact that she succeeded in putting some distance between them was only because he allowed it, and for a few seemingly long seconds she stood looking at him in stunned silence, her eyes wide and expressive as she fought for control. His gaze held an edge of mockery, and something else she dared not attempt to define.

Without a word Jake lifted a hand and trailed surprisingly gentle fingers down the length of her cheek to her jaw, then he cupped her chin and tilted it so that she had little option but to hold his gaze.

With slow deliberation he put her at arm's length. For what seemed an age he just looked at her, his eyes unfathomable depths, then he turned and walked out of the apartment.

Lisette stood in stunned silence, her gaze distant and unseeing, then she crossed slowly to the door and slid the safety-chain into place—almost as if the action would shut him out of the apartment, as well as successfully exclude him from her mind.

A resolute determination to absorb herself in her discarded notes failed dismally, and with a gesture of angry impatience she activated the television screen. After an hour of constantly switching channels she simply switched off the set and went to bed.

Sleep became an impossible escape from the tortured images swirling inside her brain, and at midnight she turned on the bedside lamp and determinedly read until four, when she slid into restless somnolence only to be haunted by dream sequences featuring a tall dark-haired figure who bore an uncanny resemblance to Adam's son.

'*Chérie*, come down for the weekend. The boutique is featuring a spring fashion parade from eleven until two on Saturday. Three models, selected guests, with canapés and champagne.'

'Maman,' Lisette voiced in token protest, 'I have paperwork coming out of my ears.'

'Dedication to work is admirable,' Louise chided, 'but to permit it to become one's master is the height of foolishness.'

'*Oui*, Maman. I stand suitably reproved.'

A light, faintly husky laugh came down the line. 'Then you will come?'

A wry smile tugged the edges of her mouth. 'How can I refuse?'

'*Excellent*. You must drive down Friday evening. We will dine out together.'

Louise, when she had made up her mind, was quite formidable, and Lisette replaced the receiver with amused resignation. She adored her mother, and valued the weekends spent on the residential peninsula situated several kilometres south of the city. Frankston was an exceedingly attractive town, its long, gently curved foreshore a scenic delight.

The boutique was Louise's pride and joy. Purchased two years ago, it was now a highly successful business venture in the centre of town, its designer stock a visual attestation to the Frenchwoman's undoubted knowledge of clothes and flair for fashion.

Lisette frequently joined Louise in the elegant salon on a Saturday morning, and she genuinely enjoyed meeting the women who bought the exclusive and outrageously expensive garments her mother displayed. Patronage had increased threefold in the past eighteen months, and a private showing of each new season's collection had proved highly successful and considered something of a social event among the wealthy residents.

A weekend away from the city would do her good, Lisette decided. Lots of clean, invigorating sea air might help clear the cobwebs from her mind. And hopefully help dispel Jake Hollingsworth's forceful image. Besides, work shouldn't be the total focus of one's life.

Friday was one of those weather-changeable days for which Melbourne was well-renowned, with intermittent squally showers followed by winds that seemed to cut through outer layers of clothes to chill the bones, and a brief glimpse of weak sunshine which was immediately replaced by dark skies heavy with the threat of imminent rain.

It was six-thirty when Lisette garaged the BMW alongside the sleek lines of her mother's hatchback.

Louise's greeting was effusive, and after a reviving cup of strong black coffee laced with a dash of brandy Lisette moved with the ease of familiarity to the bedroom her mother set aside specifically for her use, unpacked the few clothes she'd brought down with her, then she took a leisurely hot shower.

An hour later they were seated in a small local restaurant famed for its Cantonese cuisine, and after a glass of excellent Chardonnay Lisette began to relax.

'We won't linger, *chérie*, if you do not mind?' Louise spread her hands in a silent expressive gesture. 'The showing tomorrow. We will need to be at the salon early. The clothes are all pressed, the food ordered, everything is ready. But you know how it is. One must allow for any delay. And today...' she paused to effect an imperceptible shrug '...has seemed very long. *Tu comprends*?'

'Of course, Maman. I can think of nothing better than an early night.'

Louise's eyes softened as she gave her daughter a glance that revealed the full measure of her affection. 'Tomorrow evening I will make your favourite meal. Then after we have eaten we will sit before the open fire, sample a special bottle of wine, and you shall tell me all that has happened. *Oui*?'

Lisette kept her expression deliberately bland. 'You want to hear about boring affidavits and memorandums?'

'*Non, chérie*.' A musing twinkle lit Louise's eyes. 'The man in your life.'

'There is no man.'

'If you say so.'

'You're being fanciful, Maman,' she warned lightly.

'So—we talk about something else,' Louise dismissed, and Lisette caught the faint perceptive gleam evident as her mother steered the conversation into safer channels.

It was almost ten when they arrived home and, deciding not to have coffee, they retired to their respective rooms.

Saturday dawned bright and clear, yet crisply cold with the threat of another snowfall south of the Dandenong ranges. At least the rain had ceased, and with it the driving wind, Lisette determined gratefully as she followed Louise into the boutique.

It didn't take long for the ducted heating to warm the interior, and the following few hours passed quickly as Lisette worked alongside Louise in a final check of the programme, examining garments, accessories, a few last-minute phone calls, before setting out the food.

As with the preceding showings, this one proved to be a complete success. There was plenty of food and drink, the invited clientele displayed enthusiasm for every garment, and lingered long after the fashion parade to examine and buy.

Lisette handled the sales while Louise played the gracious hostess, circulating with friendly poise and uncontrived sincerity.

'I really *must* have these,' a breathy, distinctly American voice insisted, and Lisette summoned yet another smile as she relieved the owner of two very expensive designer label garments.

There was something familiar about the stunning blonde, and then recognition dawned. She had been Jake Hollingsworth's date at the restaurant on the evening Lisette had dined with Hank Preston.

The following few hours were hectic, and it was almost five when Louise ushered the last of the customers from the boutique. The models had long since departed, two assistants had dealt with numerous plates and glasses, another assistant hired for the day had restored discarded garments to their rightful position among several racks, and all that remained to be done was to collate and tally the sales dockets.

It had been a long day, but an immensely successful one, Lisette reflected as she helped Louise lock up. A leisurely shower, comfortable clothes, a glass of wine followed by one of her mother's delicious meals would provide a welcome conclusion, and she gave a faint sigh as she slid into the passenger seat.

'I have put aside a dress for the ball that is perfect for you. Consider it a gift, *chérie*,' Louise insisted as she started the car and headed towards home.

'Maman,' Lisette protested, 'if I like it, I'll buy it. You cannot keep giving me clothes.' She touched a hand to her mother's arm in a conciliatory gesture. 'Please. I insist.'

'For years while your father was ill I was unable to gift you anything. It was a struggle simply to exist.' There was a slight catch in the older woman's voice that didn't go unnoticed. 'Now that I can, you will indulge me.'

'You gave me love, and a deep sense of caring,' Lisette said gently. 'Something worth infinitely more than any material possessions.'

'Tomorrow night we will dine out. Raoul and Chiandra Carvalho insist we join them for dinner.

It matters little that you drive back to the city early Monday morning?'

They were almost home, the evening ominously dark, and the streets slick with recent rain. She could hear the faint swish of water as the tyre treads caught the excess and sent it spraying.

'If it pleases you.'

'It pleases me that you should get out more, and socialise,' Louise declared, and Lisette cast her a smile.

'I mix with plenty of people.'

'Clients. You are too young,' her mother protested gently, 'too beautiful to close yourself off from life.'

'If, by life, you allude to *men*,' Lisette ventured cynically, 'most of the ones I know would take the slightest encouragement to mean I was willing and eager to leap into their bed.'

Louise turned into the driveway, activated the remote-control module to open the garage doors, then slid the car to a halt.

'With the right man, that might not be such a bad thing.'

'Maman! You surprise me.'

'Passion, *petit enfant*, is something you should experience at least once in your lifetime.'

'I hope this preoccupation of yours doesn't indicate that you intend matchmaking.'

'*Moi*? I would not presume to do such a thing.' Louise leaned forward and pressed a light kiss to her daughter's cheek. 'Come, we will go inside and get warm, then we eat.'

The food and wine were superb, and Lisette rediscovered her appetite, finishing off the splendid meal with excellent coffee.

'I'll take care of the dishes,' she declared, rising to her feet, 'while you go through the day's receipts and prepare the banking ready for Monday.'

'*Merci*, Lisette.'

It was late when they went to bed, almost midnight, and cocooned beneath a feather-down quilt Lisette drifted off to sleep almost as soon as her head touched the pillow.

She woke to the sound of rain—a fierce, unrelenting downpour that lashed against the house in windy gusts. It was a day for staying indoors, enjoying the warmth of central heating, she determined as she slipped out of bed, showered, then joined Louise for breakfast.

Household chores took care of the morning, and after a light lunch they viewed a video, then settled down to a customary game of cards.

'Must I go with you tonight?' The thought of exchanging comfortable jeans and woollen sweater for more formal wear, drive even the shortest distance, much less conjure any degree of social vivacity, caused Lisette to proffer a faint grimace.

'*Chérie*, but of course,' Louise affirmed at once. 'Raoul and Chiandra are very good friends. They know you are down for the weekend, and they will be disappointed if you choose to stay home.'

She didn't doubt that what her mother said was true, yet she was strangely reluctant to comply. 'I could have a headache.'

'Have you?'

Fabrication was something in which she rarely indulged, and never with Louise. Inherent honesty and familial affection precluded it. 'No.'

'Then go shower and change, and we will take time to share a drink before we leave. It will brighten you spirits.'

It didn't. If anything, she felt more inclined to negate the evening entirely. Yet she forced a smile as she slid into the car beside her mother, and kept it in place as she greeted Raoul and his beautiful wife Chiandra with an innate charm not even an enemy could have faulted.

Twenty minutes later, sipping an excellent Chardonnay, she drifted into conversation with a rather innocuous young man named Jeremy, who immediately launched into a self-laudatory exposition of all his accomplishments. Although conversation wasn't exactly the right description, for he rarely gave Lisette an opportunity to voice anything more than a polite token acknowledgement to everything he said.

'Lisette. I'd like you to meet one of Raoul's associates—Charles Matheson, his wife Andrea, and their daughter Melanie.'

She turned towards Chiandra with something akin to relief, her eyes widening slightly as she recognised the curvaceous blonde standing languidly at her hostess's side.

'We've already met,' Lisette indicated with a slight smile. 'Mid-week at a restaurant, and yesterday at Louise's boutique. However, we were not introduced on either occasion.'

'Jake rarely mixes business with pleasure,' Melanie verified, shooting Lisette a veiled look of self-satisfaction.

The words held a wealth of meaning, an implication that was as clear as if they'd been lit in neon tubing for all to see. He's *mine*, was what she was really saying.

Well, Melanie was welcome to him! All that brooding power meshed with an alarming quantity of sexuality and latent passion was a volatile combination no sane woman would choose to handle.

'Jake is renewing his acquaintance with Louise,' Chiandra explained with charming ease, and Lisette forced her features to retain a seemingly unperturbed expression.

Jake was *here*?

Why shouldn't he be? she argued logically. As for engaging in conversation with her mother... Louise had no reason to bear Adam's son any grudge, and she was too gracious a lady to neglect the social niceties.

'Melanie is a model,' Chiandra elaborated, and Lisette summoned a charming smile.

'It must be an interesting occupation.'

The beautiful blonde effected a negligible shrug. 'It's a living.'

'Lisette is a lawyer.'

'Really?'

She could have been a plumber's assistant, Lisette decided, as Melanie cast her attention to the man moving towards them with familiar ease.

Louise was walking at Jake's side, and Lisette saw with veiled dismay that her mother looked as animated as if she'd re-discovered the presence of a coveted, very dear friend.

Aware that escape was impossible, she summoned a polite smile to her lips, forced by convention to accept Jake's presence with some degree of warmth. Yet her eyes were wary as she acknowledged him, shock momentarily dilating their depths as he took her outstretched hand and calmly leaned forward to brush his lips to her cheek.

CHAPTER FOUR

'LISETTE,' Jake murmured. 'How nice to see you again.'

Nice was the total antithesis of an adequate description. Without being pressed, she could think of at least three words to fling at him in vilification.

'Jake, do fetch me a drink,' Melanie almost purred, latching on to his arm in a gesture that was clearly meant to stake her claim.

'Raoul will attend to it at once,' Chiandra declared, ever the dutiful hostess, capturing her husband's attention as if by magic, and leaving Melanie to disguise a peeved pout with a helpless smile of acceptance.

'You didn't tell me you've seen Jake on several occasions since his arrival in Australia,' Louise indicated mildly, and Lisette detected her mother's speculative interest.

'Jake has chosen to employ Andersen's as his legal representative,' she revealed in an attempt to give his presence an entirely business connotation.

'You will, of course, join us for dinner one evening,' Louise extended, unaware of her daughter's desire to scream in silent vexation. 'Lisette can convey the details.'

'I'll look forward to it,' Jake accepted with the urbane charm of a practised sophisticate.

Lisette was hard pressed not to fell him with a killing glance. The need to escape, if only temporarily, was paramount, and it irked her unbearably that he knew. 'If you'll excuse me, I really must speak to Raoul,' she proffered sweetly.

Dinner was a nightmare, for whether by coincidence or design she found herself seated opposite Jake with the insipid but entirely self-obsessed Jeremy at her side.

Sheer perversity and an instinct for survival was responsible for the warmth of her interest in her immediate seating partners, and she deserved an accolade for her acting ability as she provided sparkling conversation without any apparent effort at all.

The food, however, failed to capture her attention, which was a total sacrilege, for Chiandra was a superb cook and always provided her guests with an epicurean feast.

Jake was an attentive participant, giving Louise considerable attention, much to Melanie's dissatisfaction, and Lisette seethed at his deliberate portrayal of a valued family friend. Occasionally she cast him a veiled glance, only to catch his faintly raised eyebrow in silent acknowledgement. It made her want to scream and accuse him of deliberately inveigling his way into her social life through her mother.

'What do you think, Lisette?'

She heard the words and cast Jeremy a quick glance, aware that she had not the slightest idea what he was talking about.

'I'm sure Lisette's viewpoint would have to be biased in favour of the judicial system,' Jake proffered smoothly, which only served to fuel her anger even more.

If she was going to be saved embarrassment, the last person she wanted to save her was Jake! 'It would depend whether you required a professional opinion, or a personal off-the-cuff appraisal.' Such a reply was suitably ambiguous, and successfully disguised her appalling lack of attention.

'What particular field of law are you in, Lisette?' Melanie queried, her exquisite blue eyes deliberately bland. 'It surely can't be anything as deadly dull as conveyancing?'

'I don't think I'm emotionally equipped to deal with the courtroom,' Lisette ventured evenly. 'Protagonists and pragmatism disguised in legalese simply isn't my style.'

'Shall we move into the lounge?' Chiandra suggested with her customary charm.

Coffee was served at ten, and it was almost eleven when Louise indicated they must leave. Lisette's relief was almost palpable, and it wasn't until the car was in motion that she was able to physically relax.

'A pleasant evening, *chérie. Oui*?'

Lisette possessed a definite reluctance to discuss anything regarding the previous few hours, and Jake Hollingsworth's presence in particular. '*Oui*, Maman.' She kept her gaze fixed on the dark shapes beyond the windscreen. Reflection from street-lighting cast long shadows from trees and shrubs, giving them an eerie shape that was almost menacing.

Sagely, Louise chose to keep any further observations to herself, and once home she simply brushed her lips against Lisette's cheek and bade her goodnight.

In the morning, just as Lisette was about to fire the car's engine prior to her drive back to the city, Louise tapped the window, and when Lisette wound the window down Louise leaned forward, her breath forming a hazy puff against the cold winter air.

'When you next speak with Jake, suggest he dine with us one evening next week. Friday, if that is suitable. You will drive down together, *oui*?'

There was no real time to argue or voice any protest, Lisette decided with resignation.

'I'll ring you tonight, Maman.'

When she did, she'd explain that, while Louise must feel free to invite whom she liked to dinner whenever she pleased, she, Lisette, would not be made to feel beholden to attend. Especially when Jake Hollingsworth was an intended guest.

The remainder of the week proved uneventful, the days filled with increased paperwork associated with prospective Hollingsworth International acquisitions, and Lisette enjoyed the challenge of checking every single detail before submitting the relevant documentation to Leith Andersen for final analysis. Whatever else Jake Hollingsworth held against her, she was determined he would be able to find no fault with her professional ability.

There was no contact whatsoever from Jake, although Hank Preston called her on at least three occasions regarding one specific property, and chose to impart that Jake was on the Gold Coast and not expected back in Melbourne until Friday.

The news brought a sense of relief, although as the weekend drew close she became unaccountably

angry with herself for an increase in nervous
tension.

Saturday dawned bright and clear, and Lisette
devoted the morning to visiting a nearby shopping
complex to stock up on groceries and other essen-
tials. The afternoon was spent completing several
chores in the apartment.

Tonight she was due to attend a dinner with
Louise which was being held in an inner-city restaurant to aid raising funds for cancer research, and
she showered, then dressed with care in a deep
electric-blue gown that displayed her diminutive
frame to stunning advantage.

Matching shoes and evening-purse completed the
outfit, and she took one last look at her make-up
before crossing into the lounge to await her
mother's arrival.

Five minutes later she opened the door and em-
braced the slim, slightly taller older woman who
was almost her mirror image.

'Maman,' Lisette greeted, 'you look so elegant.'

'So, chérie, do you,' Louise returned with a
warm, gracious smile. 'I shall put my overnight bag
in the spare room, then we shall leave, non?'

Some thirty minutes later they entered the restaurant and slowly moved through milling guests
towards their allocated table.

It promised to be a successful evening, Lisette
decided as her gaze swung slowly round the crowded
restaurant. The charity committee would be pleased
that their monthly function had garnered such a
dignified patronage. A prestigious social function,
it provided the gathering of society matrons with
an opportunity to display designer gowns and ex-

pensive jewellery as a visual attestation to their individual wealth and status within the community.

The evening promised to live up to its previous precedents, Lisette reflected as kisses, hugs, introductions were exchanged as a prerequisite to an interchange of the latest gossip. Without doubt during dinner, when set seating arrangements demanded an even mix of the sexes, the women would openly flirt with men who were not their husbands, who in turn would remain superficially attentive while allowing a roving eye a circumspect rein. As the evening progressed and alcohol loosened both tongues and inhibitions, it became an amusing comedy for those few of the guests who opted for total sobriety.

Each of the rectangular tables seated twelve, and Lisette was engaged in conversation when the remaining four guests arrived.

'Good evening.'

The sound of that slightly accented American drawl sent goose-bumps scudding over the surface of her skin, and she consciously dampened a surge of complex emotions as she turned and acknowledged his greeting.

Jake, who surely had to have been invited by Louise to have obtained not only tickets to this event, but to have acquired seating at the same table. Andrea and Charles Matheson, and their daughter Melanie.

Louise, when Lisette spared her a quick telling glance, smiled ever so graciously and didn't bat so much as an eyelid as she guided them into their nominated seats. Jake saw Melanie seated to his left before taking the empty chair beside Lisette.

Andrea and Charles Matheson were seated directly opposite.

Lisette knew it to be a conspiracy, although who should carry the blame was entirely debatable.

The tall model looked absolutely stunning, her deep emerald gown a perfect foil for her beautiful features and elaborate hairstyle.

Lisette felt positively plain by comparison, although any observer could have opined that her petite frame and captivating smile held infinite appeal. The deep electric-blue gown she'd elected to wear was strapless with an off-the-shoulder band to enhance its style. The bodice hugged her slender curves to the waist, then clung lovingly over her hips to finish at a fashionable length below her knees. With her hair styled into an elaborate knot atop her head from which a few tendrils had been deliberately teased loose to touch each bare shoulder, she portrayed a pleasing mixture of fragility and elegance.

A DJ presided over an elaborate electronic system positioned tastefully in one corner of the room, and soft music provided a pleasing background to the muted voices of guests.

The first course was served, then removed, and Lisette declined wine in favour of mineral water, deliberately engaging Andrea Matheson in conversation in an attempt to ignore Jake's arresting presence.

Attired in a dark formal evening suit, he looked the epitome of an urbane sophisticate, although mere words seemed inadequate to describe the striking mesh of animalistic sensuality and compelling authority he managed to exude without any effort at all.

The main course was exquisitely presented, and Lisette merely picked at it abstractedly, her appetite reduced to negligible interest as she endeavoured not to allow his close proximity to prove a disturbing factor.

A hollow laugh rose and died in her throat. Who was she kidding? He alternately provoked, angered and enraged her in a manner that frequently took her beyond the brink of rationality.

'Would you care to dance, Louise?'

Lisette heard Jake's request, followed by her mother's acceptance, and she smiled at them both as they moved out on to the dance-floor.

They looked good together, she decided, following their movements as they circled the floor. Jake attentive, courteous and perfectly at ease, and her mother easily among one of the most elegant women in the room.

'Jake simply isn't your style,' a light voice advised, and Lisette brought her gaze back to the table.

'Melanie, whatever made you think I might consider that he could be?'

'It may suit him to mix business with pleasure——' her red painted nails traced the cut pattern on the stem of her glass '—but don't let him break your heart. When his business is complete, he'll move on without so much as a backward glance.'

'You know him so well?'

Melanie's eyes held the brilliance of sapphire, and her smile was definitely feline. 'Well enough, darling.'

'How fortunate for you,' Lisette offered with dignified calm, and Melanie's teeth snapped together like a shark moving in for the kill.

'Older men are *your* speciality, aren't they? Rich old men, preferably widowers, who can be persuaded to gift you a slice of their assets before conveniently passing on to a higher plane.'

The colour drained from Lisette's cheeks, and for one infinitesimal second her eyes became stricken with pain before she successfully masked their expression.

Melanie's gaze swept assessingly over Lisette's features, noting their marked pallor with a tiny smile of victory. 'I wonder if Jake is aware your dear departed husband was in his mid-sixties?'

But *darling*, Lisette wanted to respond, he already knows, and pondered Melanie's reaction should she discover Jake was Adam's son. She was a bitch, Lisette decided silently. A cruel, vicious bitch who had obviously delved deep into the gossip grapevine to elicit her facts.

'I don't imagine Jake is in the least interested,' she managed coolly. 'Our relationship is based entirely on business.'

Melanie's smile widened. 'Of course. I didn't imagine it to be otherwise.'

If she stayed another second she'd be hard pressed not to say something regrettable. 'I think I'll go powder my nose,' she indicated, collecting her evening-purse as she rose to her feet.

'Wise of you, Lisette. Jake is escorting your dear mother back to the table at this very minute.'

Louise, ever the doting parent, exclaimed at her daughter's pallor, and Lisette's invented excuse of a headache brought forth a faint puzzling frown.

'You rarely get headaches, *chérie*. Maybe it was something you ate?'

'Perhaps. I'll take an aspirin.' She proffered a slight smile. 'If you'll excuse me for a few minutes?'

Jake's eyes were dark and unfathomable, and lingered too long on her carefully schooled features. 'If it gets worse, I'll organise a car to take you home.'

Such solicitude was almost too much. 'I'm sure that won't be necessary.'

It was a relief to escape, and she didn't care that the powder-room was crowded, or that ten minutes elapsed before she re-joined Louise at their table.

'How are you feeling, *chérie*?'

'Considerably better, Maman.'

'Can I get you something to drink?'

Lisette turned her head at the sound of Jake's deep drawling voice, and held his gaze with equanimity. 'Not at the moment.'

His faint smile did strange things to her equilibrium, and she silently damned the traitorous reaction he seemed able to evoke. It was mad to feel she needed to monitor each and every breath in an attempt to still the increased beat of her heart. Crazy to be so aware of him.

With determined effort she embarked on a conversation with her mother, discussing the merits of fashion and soliciting an opinion as to which

Australian designer was responsible for the exquisite gown worn by a well-known society matron.

'Would you like to dance?'

She wanted to say no. Yet to decline would appear uncharitable and rude, and she refused to give him the satisfaction of knowing she was afraid of being held in his arms.

'Thank you.' Her voice was gracious and polite, and she missed the faint speculative gleam in Louise's eyes as Jake led her on to the floor.

His hold was within the bounds of convention—although only just—and when another couple moved too close he caught her against him and kept her there.

'Must you?'

'Relax,' Jake drawled. 'What harm do you imagine you'll possibly come to on a dance-floor in a room full of people?'

Harm? She felt endangered every time he came near her!

'What did Melanie say to upset you?'

Dear heaven, did nothing escape him? She effected a faint shrug and concentrated on not missing her step. 'It really doesn't matter.'

'Melanie's father holds a managerial position within my company, and the family transferred to Melbourne six weeks ago.' His voice held a faint edge of cynicism. 'She has yet to meet and make the kind of friends who enjoy the lifestyle she assures her parents she cannot live without.'

Doubtless practising her feminine wiles on Daddy's boss, and loving every minute of his attention, Lisette added silently.

'Do you act as willing partner to all the daughters of your managerial staff?'

'I take a general interest in all my employees,' he drawled.

She took a deep breath and withheld a veiled response. 'What comes next? The weather? Or business? Your next prospective purchase, perhaps?'

'I have an option on a house in Toorak. The details will be on your desk Monday morning.'

'You don't waste time,' she said shakily. 'Dare I ask if it's part of your overall investment package?'

'You could say that.' His drawl was pure silk and sent shivers scudding down the length of her spine. 'I've decided to acquire it for personal use.'

Her heart tripped its beat and began to thud—so loudly, she was sure he must feel it. 'Your apartment is sufficiently spacious to entertain in.'

'Adequate, but hardly suitable as a permanent residence.'

Her voice remained locked in her throat for several timeless seconds. 'I wasn't aware you intended Melbourne to be anything other than a temporary base.'

'For the next few years my time will be divided equally between the States and Australia.'

It was more than she could do to meet his gaze, and she fell into silence, only to be jerked out of it by his softly taunting, 'No comment, Lisette?'

'Shall we go back to the table?' she countered evenly.

They were almost there when someone called her name, and she turned, her face lighting up with pleasure as she recognised a fellow law student whom she hadn't seen for more than a year.

'Alex! How are you?'

Tall, lean and impossibly loose-limbed, he was one of the most humorous, down-to-earth young men she'd ever met.

'Sweetheart, you look sensational.' He suddenly became aware of the man at her side, and his warm brown eyes surveyed Jake with undisguised thoroughness, tempering the appraisal with a satisfied smile. 'And this is?'

'Jake Hollingsworth,' she introduced quickly, following it with a generous laugh. 'He's a friend of the family,' she elaborated, watching the comic expression on Alex's mobile features.

'More than a friend, surely?' Jake intimated smoothly, slanting an enquiring eyebrow towards Alex, who promptly held out his hand.

'Alex Xenides.' He offered an engaging grin. 'Will you object if I dance with Lisette? I've only recently returned to Melbourne from more than a year in Cairns. We have some catching up to do.'

'Afterwards you might care to join us,' Jake invited smoothly. 'Everyone seems to be mixing and mingling.'

'Thanks. Just for a while. I'm with the parents and a few friends.'

Lisette bore Jake's swift scrutiny as he excused himself and made his way back to the table.

'How's life treating you these days?' Alex gave her a lop-sided smile as he caught her close and began circling the floor to the slow, lilting music. 'Aside from your absorption with conveyancing.'

'Personally?'

His eyes gleamed with devilish humour. 'Of course *personally*. If Jake Hollingsworth isn't the current man in your life, I hope to be able to sway you into having lunch with me. Or dinner. Or both.'

Lisette proffered a winsome smile. 'Still the same Alex.'

'Still besotted with you, yes.'

'Stop teasing,' she admonished, her lips curving into a wide smile as he feigned surprise.

'How do you know I'm not serious?'

'Because I shared lectures with you for three years!'

'Ah, but in those days there was too much profundity and not enough levity.' His head dipped low to rest close to hers. 'So, tell me. Who is Jake?'

With Alex there could only be honesty. 'Jake is Adam's son.'

'Hollingsworth. I should have made the connection.' His lips brushed her forehcad. 'Don't let him devour you.'

She moved away from him slightly, and her eyes were remarkably solemn as she met his steady gaze. 'He's in Australia on business.'

His smile held wry humour. 'Is that what he told you?'

'I'm handling a wealth of paperwork to prove it.'

'Be careful, Lisette. The man emanates an aura of formidable power. I wouldn't like to see you hurt.'

'There's no possibility of that happening.'

'I hope not,' he said gently. 'For your sake.'

The music swung into a fast beat, and Lisette shook her head. 'Shall we go back?'

Alex sat at their table for ten minutes, charming Louise without effort and managing to field Melanie's deliberately arch conversation with detached humour. As he left, he brushed his lips to Lisette's cheek and pressed a hand to her shoulder.

'I'll be in touch,' he assured her.

It was midnight when Louise indicated they should leave, and almost one when Lisette brought the car to a smooth halt in the apartment-block car park.

Within minutes the lift transported them swiftly to the seventh floor, and Lisette breathed a silent sigh of relief that the evening was over.

CHAPTER FIVE

THE house Jake had taken an option on was situated in one of the most exclusive streets in Toorak, and a slight frown creased Lisette's brow as she checked the formal agreement to determine the vendor's name.

Faint surprise widened her eyes. The owners were well-known for their generosity to charity, permitting use of their palatial home for a number of social functions held to raise funds for worthwhile organisations throughout the year.

A gracious two-storeyed Victorian-style mansion, it featured an abundance of cast-iron lacework, its solid interior timber work of cedar and Brazilian mahogany with floors of Italian marble covered with expensive oriental rugs.

The price-tag just had to be astronomical, she reasoned, scanning down to the figure listed, and found it far more impressive than she expected.

What on earth did Jake want with such an imposing residence? Full-time staff were required to maintain the interior and the grounds and, even given the wealth and prestige of Hollingsworth International, the home was much too large for one man alone.

Unless he was contemplating marriage and family, or seeking an entrée into Melbourne society. Or both.

Somehow the thought chilled the blood in her veins and weighted her bones. She didn't want him—she couldn't, she told herself wearily. Despite the inexplicable magnetic meshing of the emotional senses, he was the antithesis of everything she would consciously seek in a man.

A devilish imp silently cited the spellbinding interplay of emotions as a reason for the attraction—her subconscious self courting danger and excitement.

Stormfire. Violent, passionate, destructive. A wilful desire to participate in a total conflagration of all the senses.

She had to be mad to even contemplate it. Such a course was totally insane. Yet against her will she was being swept closer to the mesmeric lick of flame, hypnotised by the thrall of one man's sensual sexuality. If she had any sense, she'd walk away *now*.

Systematically, Lisette perused the relevant paperwork associated with Jake's proposed purchase, made notations, effected several phone calls, assembled all the pertinent details ready for collation and presentation to Leith Andersen.

Lunch was a hastily eaten sandwich and two cups of coffee at her desk, and it was after five when she took the elevator down to the car park.

The phone was ringing as she unlocked the door of her apartment, and she hurried to answer its insistent summons.

'Lisette? How about dinner and a movie? I'll pick you up in half an hour?'

Alex Xenides. Kind, uncomplicated, and just the person she needed to take her mind off Jake Hollingsworth.

'Love to,' she agreed without reservation. Suddenly the world seemed much brighter, and she smiled as she made a quick call to her mother.

She was putting the finishing touches to her make-up when the intercom buzzed, and she caught up her bag, identified Alex on the audio-visual monitor, then made her way to the lift.

Alex enveloped her in a bear-hug the instant she reached the lobby, then he took hold of her hand and led her out to his car. They talked non-stop en route to the city, and all through dinner. Reminiscing about fellow students, law school—*life*, and how it had affected them individually during the last two years.

The movie was a wonderful comedy which made her laugh. She was still laughing as they emerged from the cinema on to the street.

'Coffee?' Alex queried. 'There's an excellent little bar not far from here.'

'Why not?' She didn't feel in the least tired, and besides, it wasn't all that late.

'I'll have you home by midnight.' Alex gave an infectious grin. 'Just like Cinderella, before my very functional vehicle turns into a pumpkin.'

'You've mixed up the story,' Lisette teased.

'So I have,' he said gravely. 'Does it matter?'

'The way you tell it, you can't play the prince.'

'Ah,' he accorded with comical solemnity, 'but then I was never meant to.'

'Perhaps you get to be the prince in *Sleeping Beauty*,' she consoled, and he smiled.

'That's the problem.' He reached out and caught hold of her hand. 'We're both in different fables.'

It was as if the last three years didn't exist, Lisette decided as they found a small table in the corner and placed their order. A sense of *déjà vu* persisted as they sipped the aromatic black coffee. How many cups of coffee had they shared? Between lectures, to soothe fractured pre-exam nerves, coffee to keep awake for the long hours of studying far into the night.

'Can we repeat this, do you think?' Alex queried as he settled the bill.

'Yes, of course.' She should get out more. To-night had been a wonderfully warm, relaxing experience.

Alex brought the car to a halt in the wide sweeping apron adjacent to the main entry into the apartment block.

'Should I attempt to kiss you?'

'A friendly salute to my cheek?' Lisette teased lightly.

'Oh, definitely brotherly,' he agreed, and leaning forward he brushed his lips across hers before reaching forward to unclasp her door.

As she emerged a car drew level then swept on its way down to the underground car park, and a pulse started hammering in her throat as she rec-ognised the sleek Jaguar with Jake behind the wheel.

There was no reason to feel apprehensive, so why did her nerves feel on edge and as taut as a tightly stretched piece of wire?

Summoning a brilliant smile, she bade Alex goodnight, closed the car door, then walked briskly through the main entrance, used her coded key to gain access to the lobby, and moved towards the lifts to jab the call-button with more than necessary force.

A minute later the doors slid open, and she felt a chill shiver slither down the length of her spine as her eyes swept to Jake's tall frame positioned indolently at ease inside the lift.

'Are you coming inside?'

Said the spider to the fly, she finished silently, knowing she was equally damned whether she entered or not. The butterflies inside her stomach spread their wings and began an agitated tattoo, making her want to scream out in angry rejection as she consciously fought for control.

Without a word she stepped forward, and there was no power on earth to prevent the trapped feeling that assailed her, nor an acute awareness of his presence.

'Did you have an enjoyable evening?'

Anger lent her eyes a fiery sparkle, and she tilted her chin in defiance as she met his dark, sardonic gaze. 'Did you?'

Something flared in his eyes, and he regarded her in silence for several heart-stopping seconds. 'What's the matter, Lisette?' he queried silkily. 'Xenides disappoint you?'

She looked at him carefully, aware of the aura of strength, the indolent sophistication. 'Alex is a friend.'

'And you don't make lovers of friends?'

The slow anger that had been simmering away inside her for far too long erupted into fiery rage. 'That was uncalled for.'

'Indeed?'

His cynical drawl was the living end, and she turned towards the instrument panel. 'Damn you! I'll stop the elevator and take another!'

He reached out and captured her wrist with galling ease, then tugged her gently forward.

'What the hell do you think you're doing?' She began to struggle, flailing against him as he impelled her into his arms, and there was little she could do to avoid his descending head as he sought her mouth with his own.

A despairing moan scorched her throat, unable to find voice as he wreaked havoc with her tortured emotions in a kiss that was the antithesis of anything she'd previously experienced.

Against her will she became caught up in the wild, sweet hunger that rose from deep within. She was on fire, every nerve-end alive with vibrant life, and a shudder shook her slender frame, an almost convulsive reaction to the traitorous kindling of desire that swept like flame through her body.

It was crazy to feel like this, to be so intensely aware that it was almost as if she'd been waiting a lifetime for this one man's touch, she thought dazedly as at last he lifted his head and pushed her to stand at arm's length.

There had been a vague cruelty apparent, a hard mercilessness that sought to overwhelm in a way she would find impossible to forget.

Lisette was intensely conscious of him, his dark, chiselled profile, the unfathomable depths of his eyes, and she wasn't capable of uttering so much as a word as he reached out a hand and depressed a button on the instrument panel.

The doors whispered open, and the sound brought their whereabouts sharply into focus.

'Your floor,' Jake drawled, and her eyes filled with pain at his cynicism, then she masked the hurt and walked into the vestibule without so much as a backward glance.

Inside her apartment she carefully locked the door, then she undressed and slid into bed to lie staring at the darkened ceiling as she willed sleep in an attempt to escape Jake's forceful image.

In a deliberate attempt to bury herself in her work, Lisette refused any social invitations and spent every evening studying a weighty tome she'd acquired several months previously and hadn't so much as opened its tooled leather cover.

Consequently she went late to bed and woke feeling drained and depleted, both physically and emotionally.

Friday morning the insistent peal of the telephone penetrated Lisette's subconscious mind, and she instinctively reached out for the handset on the nearby bedside pedestal.

'*Chérie*, did I wake you?' It was Louise, sounding unduly concerned that her daughter should still be in bed, and Lisette spared a quick glance at her watch, then rose abruptly into a sitting position. It was almost eight, and she should have already showered and dressed and lingered over coffee.

'Maman, what is it? I'll have to rush.' There would be no time for breakfast, or even coffee, and she'd have to fly like the wind if she was to reach the office on time.

'I will bring the dress for you to wear tonight. It is perfection. *You*,' Louise asserted.

Tonight? Then realisation dawned. The annual ball for one of her mother's two favoured charities was to be held in the ballroom of one of the city's most prestigious hotels.

A tireless committee member for two prominent charities, Louise gave much of her time and effort to helping raise much needed funds for medical research. Social luncheons, fashion parades were merely a few functions in which she actively participated, and the ball numbered as one of the year's highlighted social events.

'You had not forgotten, surely, *chérie*?'

'No, of course not.'

'Jacqueline will be driving, so we will both return to Frankston tonight. We will be at the apartment about seven to collect you.'

'*Merci*, Maman. Have a nice day.'

As soon as she replaced the receiver, Lisette leapt out of bed, took a quick shower, then hurriedly dressed and drove into the city.

Contrary to Louise's injunction, Lisette's day became fraught with problems. Last-minute delays on two settlements, which involved a series of phone calls, an irate client, and, worse, her usual stenographer had called in sick and she was forced to use a junior typist who had just joined the firm and proved to be unfamiliar with legal terminology.

Lunch was something she sent out for and ate at her desk, and Hank Preston's call requesting priority on pressing documentation didn't augur well for a tranquil afternoon.

Consequently it was a relief to leave the office at the end of the day and drive home to the relative serenity of her apartment.

Opting for a leisurely soak instead of a shower, she filled the spa-bath, added essence, then she stripped her clothes and sank into the scented hot water, closing her eyes with contemplated bliss as the gently pulsing jets soothed and eased the tenseness from her body.

Thirty minutes later she emerged to towel herself dry, then, her toilette complete, she donned fresh underwear, slipped into a robe, and began applying her make-up.

At precisely seven Louise utilised her own key to enter the apartment, and Lisette greeted Jacqueline with the customary brush of her lips to each cheek before proffering both women a genuine compliment for the exquisite gowns they had chosen to wear.

'I have brought yours, *chérie*,' Louise indicated, presenting Lisette with a protective dress-bag. 'Now go and change, then we will be on our way.'

The gown was a stunning creation in deep red figure-hugging velvet. Strapless, the bodice was cunningly swathed to accent her tiny waist, draped across her hips, then fell in fluid folds to ankle-length. Long red gloves and matching handmade high-heels completed the outfit, and Lisette added a slim patterned gold choker and fixed diamond studs to each ear.

Her mirrored image reflected the smooth perfection of her skin, the wide-spaced hazel eyes deep, fathomless pools that reflected unblinking solemnity as they viewed the glossy sable of her hair worn upswept in a simple twist that served to emphasise her slender neck.

A generous spray of perfume—her favourite Dior—and she was ready.

'Exquisite,' Louise and Jacqueline breathed in unison, and Lisette smiled in response, then collected her evening-purse and indicated they should leave.

The ball was attended by the cream of society with nearly all of the tickets pre-sold, and those remaining were quickly snapped up as society doyennes planned their calendar and their wardrobe in an effort to be *seen* at one of the year's major social events.

Lisette glanced around the huge room the hotel had allocated for the venue, and estimated there were at least three hundred guests present. Taking an occasional sip from her glass of champagne, she offered a faint smile when Jacqueline indicated a need to check some minor detail with another committee member.

'Thank you for the gown, Maman,' she murmured quietly. 'As always, you have impeccable taste.'

'My pleasure, *chérie*. In it, you look breathtakingly beautiful.'

Lisette accepted the compliment, and returned it with warm sincerity, before asking, 'When do you leave for Sydney?'

'Next Saturday. I am really looking forward to it.'

'It's so long since you last took a holiday. You should make it two weeks instead of one.'

Louise effected a light shrug. 'Perhaps I may take another week towards the end of the year. It depends on the boutique. You know how it is.'

'Louise, Lisette.'

Lisette turned at the sound of that deep, drawling voice, and felt the familiar unfurling of nervous tension begin deep inside. What the *hell* was Jake doing here? Yet why shouldn't he be? an inner voice taunted.

She met his dark, enigmatic gaze with equanimity, and even managed a polite greeting as Louise welcomed him with one of her warm smiles. 'I'm so pleased you could come.'

Louise *invited* him? What was this—a conspiracy?

Lisette was so consumed with anger that she barely registered a word Jake said as he took a seat immediately opposite.

'My apologies for being late.'

'Nonsense,' Louise dismissed kindly. 'You explained that it might be a possibility.'

I don't believe this, Lisette thought dully. If it wouldn't cause her mother embarrassment, she'd excuse herself and leave. Except such an action would depict her as spoilt and rude, and she was neither. Just impossibly angry that Jake seemed intent on infiltrating her life—at work, on a social level, even to the extent of using the same apartment building instead of staying in a city hotel.

It didn't make sense. *None* of his actions made sense. Unless he was attempting a cruel game of revenge by attempting to involve her emotions, use and abuse them, thereby contriving to cause her pain.

Power and ruthlessness went hand in hand, and there could be no doubt that he possessed both qualities. It wasn't inconceivable that he might deliberately utilise sexual chemistry and sensual expertise as a diabolical weapon against her.

She wouldn't allow him to win. Nor would she give him the slightest satisfaction of even thinking he might succeed. All she had to do was remain politely aloof, refuse all of his invitations, and keep any contact on a strictly business footing.

Which was all very well, she decided a few hours later when he calmly outmanoeuvred her attempt to refuse joining him on the dance-floor, but the crazy thing was that he *knew* how she felt, and he simply overrode her resistance with a display of dispassionate inflexibility that made her incredibly resentful.

'You don't *have* to dance with me,' Lisette said fiercely. It was ridiculous to feel threatened, yet held in his arms, and despite slender-heeled evening shoes giving an added four inches in height, her eyes were only level with his impeccable black bow-tie. The result was that she felt positively caged, needing, *wanting* to rear back from him like a frightened gazelle.

'No,' Jake agreed imperturbably.

Wide golden-hazel eyes widened even further and blazed with reflected anger, she demanded, 'Then why are you?'

'Impossible that I might want to,' he drawled, and although he didn't alter his hold she felt as if the arms that held her had undergone an imperceptible change and were steel instead of muscle and bone.

'You're everywhere I go,' she flared, sorely tried. 'The office appearances are legitimate, but socially?' She drew a deep breath and expelled it slowly. 'Even my mother seems part of the collusion, selling you tickets to functions and inviting you to dinner. It isn't *fair*!'

'I don't intend for it to be fair.'

'No,' she agreed angrily. 'But I won't let you win.'

His head lowered down to hers, and his mouth hovered close to her temple. 'And I cannot conceive losing. It is a classic impasse, wouldn't you agree?'

'Then why not abandon the game and leave me alone?' Lisette beseeched.

'You must know that is an impossibility.'

His lips brushed against her ear and she reared back from his touch as if seared by flame. 'Don't do that!'

'It is not my intention to harm you.' His voice held amusement, and she was so enraged that she almost choked out the words.

'Not physically.'

'Imagining you in the physical sense is a provocative thought. Especially in bed. Do you wear silk or satin?' Jake intoned musingly. 'Or, preferably, nothing at all?'

'You'll never know!'

One eyebrow slanted in mocking humour. 'So sure, Lisette?'

'*Yes*, damn you!'

'I doubt my father will be the only man in your life.'

Her eyes flashed dark fire. 'Adam was sensitive and kind.'

His smile was totally without humour. 'You have no conception what sort of lover I am.'

A slight shiver feathered its way across her skin, raising all her fine body hairs in instinctive awareness of precisely how he would be with a woman. Unrestrained, passionate, and completely shameless.

She felt suddenly afraid for herself, for wanting to tempt the devil and dare to find out, yet desperately aware that if she did she'd never be the same again.

'It will never happen.'

'Brave words,' he drawled. 'Spoken by a woman whose head is totally at variance with the dictates of her body.'

'This time you've gone too far,' she said shakily as she attempted to wrench herself out of his arms. 'Let me go, damn you!'

His hold didn't alter. 'I suggest you leave all this fine vilification for a time when I can effectively deal with it.'

'Oh, go to *hell*.'

To her utter mortification, his mouth settled over hers in what must have appeared to any interested onlookers a lingering kiss. Only she felt the subtle hint of punishment, and the threat of what would follow when he managed to get her alone.

'You're totally despicable!' she whispered fiercely as he raised his mouth a bare inch above her own.

'Shall we attempt a partial truce?' The faintly inflected drawl held wary cynicism, and his eyes held hers with unwavering scrutiny.

Lisette drew a deep calming breath and endeavoured to still the faint feeling of fear licking along her nerves. 'I'd like to go back to the table.'

If Louise noticed anything amiss she made no comment, and for the remainder of the evening Lisette attempted to act out an expected part as she dutifully conversed with a few fellow guests. She even returned to the dance-floor with three different men, and to all appearances she gave the impression of enjoying herself.

The strain of it all gave her a headache, and she was immensely relieved when the evening drew to a close.

'We will drop you off at the apartment, *chérie*,' Louise declared, and Jake intervened smoothly,

'I'll take Lisette home.'

His smile appeared reassuringly warm, and Lisette wondered how her mother could be so taken in by him. It was useless to protest, but she said the words anyway. 'Really, I can take a taxi.'

'Nonsense,' Jake dismissed. 'I have my car, and we share the same destination.'

But not the same apartment, she longed to fling. Although after being publicly subjected to his kiss she doubted anyone would believe they hadn't at least spent some time intimately engaged in one apartment or the other.

'What an excellent solution.' Louise's smile indicated her approval. 'Thank you, Jake. I shall look forward to next Friday evening when you join us at Frankston for dinner.'

There was little Lisette could do but acquiesce and bid her mother goodnight.

In the car she sat in silence, insulated from the heated warmth by the ice that seemed to flow through her veins. Outside the night was black, with not a star in sight, and as she watched huge spots of rain began to dot the windscreen, falling with increasing frequency until Jake activated the wipers; then she became mesmerised by their constant swish as they dispersed the excess water.

Jake brought the powerful car to a halt in the underground car park, then together they rode the elevator to the seventh floor.

Lisette emerged into the vestibule, then turned briefly to bid him goodnight, only to find he had followed, and seemed intent on escorting her to the door of her apartment.

'Really, there's no need for you to play the gallant,' she uttered stiltedly, aware of a slow, burning anger that surged into life.

'I had hoped you might offer me some coffee,' he drawled, and Lisette shot him a baleful glare.

'It's late, and I'm tired.'

He took the key from her nerveless fingers and inserted it into the lock. 'Then allow me to make it for you.'

'I don't want any coffee!' It was too late to forbid him entry into the apartment, for the simple reason that he was already there.

Damn him, she silently seethed as he closed the door and moved into the lounge. He had no right to ignore her wishes, and she told him so, her eyes reflecting brilliant shards of dark golden-green.

'Don't you understand? I don't want you here!'

One eyebrow lifted in a gesture of silent mockery. 'In this apartment, or in your life?'

'*Both*!'

His eyes caught hers and held them captive, and her stomach lurched, then completed a painful somersault as his features assumed a sardonic hardness that made her feel suddenly afraid.

'Not a chance, Lisette.'

The colour fled from her face as the shock of his words registered. 'What do you mean?' she demanded in scandalised disbelief.

'I'll get to you any way I can. Through work, your friends—even your mother,' Jake declared silkily, and she looked at him with utter loathing.

'You bastard! It won't work.'

Hard cynicism darkened his eyes, and his expression assumed inflexibility as he effected a faint shrug. 'You can't retreat into total seclusion.'

'I won't let you do this to me,' she said fiercely.

'How do you propose to stop me?'

Temper flared forth in a brilliant explosion of wrath. 'Go to hell!'

She was so enraged that she didn't give a thought to stilling her hand as it flew towards his face, and she gave a cry of pain as he caught it in a crushing grip only inches from its objective.

For several long seconds her angry gaze locked with his, and she almost died at the chilling intensity evident on his taut features.

'*Why*?' she demanded in a tortured voice. 'What have I ever done to deserve this?'

'You make it sound like an annihilation of your soul,' Jake drawled, thwarting every effort she made to struggle free of him.

His words were chillingly accurate, and for several long seconds she simply looked at him in silence. 'Let me go.' She hadn't meant to beg. Her eyes felt large, and she blinked to dispel the vague ache apparent within them. 'Please.'

His hands shifted to curve over her shoulders. 'You resorted to hitting me once before,' he reminded in an inflexible drawl. 'This time I don't feel quite so generous.'

His intention was obvious, and she cursed herself for daring to incite his anger. To struggle against his sheer strength was futile, and in a desperate bid to avoid his mouth she twisted her head to one side only to discover he had already anticipated such a move.

His lips were hard and cruel as they crushed hers, his tongue an unrelenting instrument that made her cry out in silent antipathy as he deepened the kiss, taking, possessing in a manner that was totally alien to anything she'd ever experienced.

Yet beneath the searing subjugation was an element of restrained emotion that made her feel almost afraid. Not of him, but of her own traitorous emotions.

For one totally crazy moment she wanted to melt against his muscle-hard frame, to lift her arms and entwine them round his neck, to temper all his controlled anger and tame it into shameless passion. The knowledge shocked her and, almost as if he knew, the pressure of his mouth eased and took on a persuasive quality, a depth of feeling that promised almost as much as it provoked.

The arms that bound her to him no longer felt like imprisoning steel, and she knew she should tear her mouth away from his before it was too late.

Yet even as she hesitated she knew she'd left it far too long, that her quiescence damned her as equally as if she'd returned his embrace.

What followed left her weak-willed and totally malleable as he led her into a dangerous abyss where sheer emotion ruled and rational thought escaped way beyond her reach.

Absorbed was the only adequate word that came to mind, and somewhere deep inside she began to ache with the knowledge that she'd never be able to withstand this man's total possession and survive intact.

It seemed an age before he slowly lifted his head, and she could only look at him in silence, her eyes enmeshed in the darkness of his as she fought to regain some semblance of sanity.

Her entire being felt as if it were about to fragment into a thousand pieces, and she was conscious of an inner fragility as she closed her eyes briefly against the compelling sight of him.

Her mouth felt swollen, and she unconsciously began a tentative seeking exploration over the fullness of her lower lip with the tip of her tongue, only to lower her gaze in protective self-defence as she glimpsed the darkness in his own and the slight flaring that made her feel incredibly afraid.

Firm fingers lifted her chin and, standing quite still, she bore his silent scrutiny until every nerve tautened with pain. With incredible gentleness he traced the soft contours of her mouth with the pad of his thumb, and her lips trembled beneath his touch.

Damn. Tears welled of their own volition, and she blinked to dispel the watery mist, allowing the lids to flutter down in desperation against the threatening spill.

Lisette felt his hands shape each side of her face an instant before his mouth covered hers, and this time his kiss was a tantalising expiation that alternately savoured and offered a hypnotic seduction.

Then she was free, and she stood in silence, her eyes widening slightly beneath his vital, vibrant gaze. For a few heart-stopping seconds she was mesmerised, unable to hide the haunting vulnerability she felt, and it took considerable effort to lower her hands from his shoulders and step away from him.

Jake's eyes were strangely watchful as they witnessed the subtle play of emotions chasing across her expressive features, and she tore her gaze away from the firm curve of his mouth.

He was so darned *invincible*. How could he stand there looking so controlled, when she was a mass of trembling nerves and unable to assemble one coherent thought?

'I think you'd better leave.' Her voice sounded impossibly husky, almost indistinct, and she hated herself almost as much as she hated *him*.

'Would it be so very bad if I stayed?'

He could defeat her on two fronts—with the use of sheer physical strength, or by utilising all the sensual expertise at his command. Either way, she wouldn't stand a chance, and they both knew it.

'I'd never forgive you if you did.'

She watched in fascination as he lifted a hand and trailed his fingers across her cheek, then traced the line of her jaw and lingered at the edge of her mouth.

'Goodnight.'

Without a further word he turned and walked to the front door, opened it, then closed it quietly behind him.

Lisette made her way slowly to her bedroom and began to undress, then she donned a silk nightgown and removed her make-up before slipping wearily into bed.

There were too many chaotic thoughts scattering inside her head to allow an easy slide into restful somnolence, and it was close to dawn when she fell into a fitful doze, only to awaken to the sound of the telephone.

'Good morning, *chérie*.' Louise—her voice serene and sympathetically kind. 'I thought I would ring before leaving for the boutique. Are you coming down this weekend?'

A quick glance at the bedside clock revealed it to be eight-thirty, and Lisette uttered a faint groan. Why did it feel as if it were the middle of the night?

'*Oui*, Maman.' She sat up and ran fingers through the length of her hair. 'But please, no entertaining. Perhaps tomorrow we could drive to the mountains and enjoy some time in the snow. Just the two of us.'

Which was precisely what transpired, and after a peaceful weekend Lisette rose early Monday morning, donned a warm tracksuit, then took a long leisurely walk along the beachfront at dawn.

The weather was cold and blustery, the bay bleak and grey, its surface a wind-tossed mass. Every now and then she paused to watch a pair of keening gulls soar down on to the sandy foreshore and fossick for scraps. Their cries sounded oddly human, and as she approached they took flight, dipping low out over the water as they circled in towards the edge of the incoming tide.

At this hour of the morning there was an air of tranquillity, a feeling of being one with the elements, and she lifted her face, letting the strong, blustery wind whip at her hair.

After a while she turned and retraced her steps, reaching her mother's home just as huge splashes of rain rent the air.

A long hot shower, followed by breakfast, then she changed into a tailored suit, bade Louise an affectionate farewell, and slid into her car to drive into the city.

CHAPTER SIX

IT WAS eight-thirty when Lisette entered the reception area at Andersen's, and she viewed the papers already on her desk in silent dismay.

For the next few hours she worked at an enviable pace, making and taking phone calls as she systematically dealt with her assigned work.

The peal of the phone disturbed her concentration, and Lisette reached for the receiver automatically, intoning a professional response as she slipped a marker into the file she'd been studying.

'Alex Xenides, Lisette. How about dinner?' His voice held infectious humour, and she found herself smiling in response.

'When?'

'Tonight?'

A faint laugh bubbled to the surface at his overt eagerness. 'This is short notice.'

'Shall we say six-thirty?'

'Do you mind if it's just dinner? I'd prefer not to have a late night.'

'I can have you home as early as you want,' came his cheerful reply, and she agreed before replacing the receiver with a feeling of pleasurable anticipation.

Alex was charming, kind, and uncomplicated. An evening in his company would be no hardship at all.

An hour later she answered the phone to discover Hank Preston on the line, and after discussing business for all of ten minutes he switched to personalities.

'Jake asked me to tell you he's booked a table for dinner tonight, and he'll collect you at seven.'

Lisette closed her eyes, then slowly opened them again. 'Tell Jake I don't accept invitations second-hand.'

'He flew to Sydney early this morning and won't be back until late afternoon,' Hank revealed wryly. 'He's involved in heavy meetings all day.'

'He has a mobile phone, and I'm sure he can take the few minutes necessary to ring me himself. In any case, tonight isn't convenient. I already have a date.'

'I'll relay that to him.'

'Please do.'

Damn Jake Hollingsworth! Who did he think he was that he could get his right-hand man to act on his behalf on a personal matter, and expect her to fall in with his plans? It was typical of his brand of arrogance.

Lisette was just about to leave the office for the day when the phone rang, and she retraced her steps to pick up the receiver.

'Lisette LeClaire.'

'Hank relayed that nothing less than a personally delivered invitation will do.' Jake's slightly accented voice drawled down the line, and her knuckles clenched white.

'I presume Hank also informed you that I've already made arrangements for this evening?' She drew a deep breath in the hope that it might steady her rapidly beating pulse. 'You'll have to excuse me, I was just on my way out.' Without a second thought she replaced the receiver, and then stood staring at it with reflected guilt.

When it started ringing again a few seconds later a sudden chill invaded her veins, cooling her temper, and she stood transfixed, wondering whether it was a totally unrelated call or Jake on the line.

She could walk away, and she nearly did, attempting to justify such an action with the knowledge that if she had immediately left the office after replacing the receiver she'd never have heard the phone ring a second time.

Damn. Reaching out, she snatched it up and identified herself.

'Don't hang up on me, Lisette,' Jake intoned with soft menace, and she shivered as the force of his magnetism emanated from him down the line.

'As far as I was concerned, our conversation had reached its conclusion,' she said with quiet vehemence. 'You might call the shots when it comes to business, but I'm on my own time now, and your call was entirely personal. At the risk of being accused of hanging up on you yet again, I'll give advance notice of my intention to end this call. Goodnight.'

Without a qualm she collected her briefcase and walked from the office into the lobby, where she summoned the lift with an unnecessarily forceful jab of the call-button. Five minutes later she slid into the BMW and drove with a sense of controlled anger through traffic-choked streets whose slow-moving progress was enough to tax the patience of a saint.

A long, leisurely shower did much to restore a sense of calm, and she selected her clothes with care, choosing a fashionably cut dress in fine emerald-green wool. Slender high-heeled black shoes and a black evening-purse completed the outfit, and she kept make-up to a minimum, colouring her mouth with a clear rose and emphasising her eyes with the subtle use of kohl and green eyeshadow. Her hair was swept up into a smooth knot, and she slung a black velvet coat across her shoulders as the intercom buzzed.

Alex's friendly features showed up on the television monitor.

'I'm on my way,' she said at once.

The lift arrived within seconds of being summoned, and her stomach clenched in painful reaction as the doors slid open to reveal Jake standing indolently at ease inside the electronic cubicle.

'Going down?'

His drawling query made all her fine body hairs rise in protective self-defence, and Lisette cursed the apprehension that slipped icily through her veins.

It was crazy to be so aware of him, to feel as if each separate nerve-ending was tautening to its furthest limitation as the door slid shut and held her captive with this unpredictable, infuriating man.

Lisette met his steady gaze with equanimity, and chose to ignore the mocking lift of his eyebrow, the knowledge that he *knew* the reason for her reservation.

She was supremely conscious of him, to such an extent that it affected her breathing and locked the power of speech in her throat. Part of her longed to force a vilifying confrontation, and to hell with the consequences.

It couldn't have taken more than fifteen seconds to reach the ground floor, but beneath Jake's intimidating, analytical appraisal it felt ten times that long, and she had to physically restrain herself from leaping out into the lobby the moment the doors slid open.

Alex, bless him, was standing only a few feet distant, and he moved forward to envelop her in a bear-like hug.

'Mm,' he murmured as he pushed her to arm's length. 'You look fantastic.'

'I have to agree.'

Alex turned at once, his expression one of speculative interest as his gaze moved from Jake to Lisette, and he inclined in head in acknowledgement of the other man's presence.

Jake's eyes portrayed lazy humour, and almost as if he sensed the younger man's train of thought he offered mockingly, 'Lisette's sense of familial duty doesn't extend to having me as her houseguest.'

Anger coloured Lisette's cheeks, and the look she cast him would have withered a lesser mortal into a state of utter speechlessness. Catching hold of Alex's arm, she turned away from Jake's disturbing gaze. 'Shall we go?'

'Enjoy your evening.'

Jake made it sound as if he were bidding two teenagers have a pleasant time, and Lisette inwardly seethed as Alex led her out through the main entrance.

'I hope you like Italian food. There's a fantastic little restaurant not too far from here.'

'Lead the way.' Lord, she sounded brittle. Even her smile seemed forced, and she wanted to scream with sheer vexation. *Damn* Jake. Damn him to hell.

On reflection it was an enjoyable night. The ambience created by the restaurant reflected a homely family kitchen, with muted Italian music, friendly staff and superb food.

Lisette couldn't remember when she'd last laughed quite so much as Alex recounted numerous anecdotes accumulated as a duty solicitor with the magistrate's court.

Consequently it was after ten when they left the restaurant and Alex drove her the short distance home.

'No invitation to join you for coffee?'

Lisette directed him a solemn look. 'I really had a great time, Alex.'

He laughed softly. 'That's the nicest refusal I've had. When will I see you again?'

'Ring me.'

He leaned forward and kissed her gently. 'You can bet on it.'

Reaching for the door-clasp, she slid out from the passenger seat and walked quickly to the building, then used her security key to enter the lobby.

Inside her apartment she locked up and made her way into the kitchen, smiling in amusement as she poured heated milk into a mug and carried it through to the lounge.

Alex was fun, and the evening had been one of the most enjoyable she had spent in a long time.

However, it wasn't his face which rose to taunt her, or the sweetness of his kiss. Other fine-chiselled, compelling features filled her vision, and her memory of Jake's mouth was the antithesis of sweet as it had sought to impress her own with the kind of relentless hunger she was ill-equipped to deal with.

Perhaps Maman was right, she brooded as she sipped the hot milk. It would be nice to have a male companion to rely on to escort her to various functions. Someone with whom she could relax.

You had that with Adam, a tiny voice taunted. But he was different, the situation unusual, almost unique, she agonised silently.

Jake was an unknown entity, his dramatic mesh of sexual sensuality a blatant elemental force from which she instinctively withdrew, afraid she'd go up in flames if she dared invite his possession.

Dear lord in heaven, what was she thinking of? She had to be mad, totally *insane* to even contemplate an alliance with such a man.

Yet steadily he was invading her life. Uttering a shaky curse, she rose to her feet in one fluid movement. He wouldn't succeed—she wouldn't let him. Coercion was against the law, and harassment was a punishable offence. If he dared suggest that they shared a relationship, she'd personally slay him!

She didn't sleep at all for what seemed like hours, and she came sharply awake at the persistent peal of her alarm tired, emotionally drained, and in possession of the grand-daddy of a headache.

Worse, an examination of her features in the bathroom mirror revealed waxen-pale cheeks, and dark smudges beneath dull, pain-filled eyes.

'*Charming*,' she groaned out loud. A hot shower, followed by toast and strong black coffee did much to improve her disposition, as did two pain-killers, although no amount of skilfully applied make-up could completely disguise the ravaging effect of emotional exhaustion.

As if that weren't enough, when she summoned the lift, who should be the sole occupant when it paused at her floor but Jake, and his unwavering scrutiny through narrowed eyes as they rode down to the underground car park was the absolute limit.

'Have you quite finished?' Lisette blazed at him in a restrained fit of temper.

'You look—bruised,' he drawled with imperturbable calm, and sheer unadulterated rage darkened her features as she sought to shock.

'Maybe I am.'

His eyes lanced hers, mocking and impossibly cynical. 'Not from a night indulging in sex games.'

'What interesting terminology you use,' she observed with biting cynicism as the elevator slid to a smooth halt.

Lisette preceded him into the basement without a further word and, totally ignoring him, she walked to where her car was parked, unlocked it and slid in behind the wheel.

Minutes later she eased the BMW into the flow of city-bound traffic, and in a bid to soothe her fractured nerves she slid a tape into the cassette deck.

The morning became fraught with numerous calls on her time, and lunch was a hastily eaten sandwich washed down with fruit juice.

Leith Andersen relayed that Jake Hollingsworth would be in Sydney until the end of the week, and Hank Preston had accompanied him.

The news should have pleased her; instead she felt strangely bereft. Immensely cross with herself, she extracted a file and systematically began making notations.

It was almost five on Friday when the phone rang for what seemed the umpteenth time that afternoon, and she threw the hapless machine a venomous look as she snatched up the receiver.

'Louise suggested we drive down to Frankston together,' Jake informed her with dangerous quietness.

'I'm not going anywhere with you.'

'Six, Lisette,' he insisted silkily, and hung up.

The dinner had quite slipped her mind, and she groaned out loud at the prospect of spending an evening in Jake's company.

She could ring her mother and plead a headache. At least it wouldn't be an untruth. Except if she didn't go, Louise would express her anxiety, and possibly empower Jake to conduct a personal check on her daughter's state of health.

It was five-thirty when she unlocked her apartment, and almost six when she was ready. In the intervening half-hour she'd taken a quick shower, then changed into an elegant lightweight cream woollen dress before tending to her make-up. Her hair was upswept into a simple twist, and when the doorbell rang she simply slid her feet into high-heeled shoes, caught up her coat, collected her bag and made for the door.

'You're ready.'

Lisette closed her eyes, then opened them again at the sight of Jake's tall frame looming large in the aperture. He portrayed raw masculinity combined with ruthless invincibility. A predictably unpredictable menace who rode roughshod over her in an unmitigated display of unconscionable arrogance.

'What did you expect?'

His smile held sardonic cynicism. 'It wouldn't have surprised me to discover you'd opted to drive down alone.'

'Only the thought of upsetting my mother prevented me from doing so,' she retorted as she moved out into the hall and locked the apartment.

There was a dangerous sense of animalistic power beneath his sheath of expensive tailoring, and she was intensely aware of him as they rode the elevator down to the basement car park.

In the confines of his car it was worse, and she sat in silence as he manoeuvred the large vehicle through traffic en route to the main highway leading south to Frankston.

The last thing she wanted or needed was an entire evening spent in his hateful company. Especially beneath the observant eye of her mother.

'Can we come to some agreement about what time we'll leave? I don't want a late night,' she said.

'I imagine not,' Jake declared drily, and she burst into angry speech.

'You're not my keeper, and you have no right to pass judgement on what I do.'

'I doubt you'll come to any harm with Alex Xenides.' His voice had an infinite degree of cynicism, and she drew in an angry breath, then released it slowly in an attempt to hold on to her temper.

'No,' she agreed stiltedly. '*You*, however, are an entirely different matter.'

He slanted her a mocking glance. 'At least you recognise it.'

'Oh, for heaven's sake!' Her hands clenched together until the knuckles shone white, and her palms hurt as her nails dug into them. 'This whole débâcle is impossible. *You're* impossible!' Stupid ignominious tears stung her eyes, and she blinked to stem their flow.

The evening could only be a disaster, and yet there was nothing she could do about it. Even if she asked, Jake was unlikely to turn the car and take her back to her apartment, and she'd never come up with a suitable explanation to appease Louise.

She felt incredibly fragile, and her temples throbbed with the onset of a headache. Wearily she leaned back against the headrest and closed her eyes, unaware of the sharp, faintly brooding glance she incurred as the Jaguar sped smoothly towards its destination.

All too soon the car slowed and drew to a halt, and Lisette gave a start as a hand closed over hers.

'Louise has seen us arrive,' Jake warned quietly.

Summoning a smile, she slid out from the car and into her mother's welcoming embrace before stepping indoors, aware of Louise's light voice mingling with Jake's deeper tones as they followed her into the house.

It was a tremendous relief to discover Louise had invited three other guests and, after enjoying a predinner drink, Lisette escaped into the kitchen on the pretext of helping her mother.

'*Chérie*,' Louise protested, 'almost everything is ready. All I have to do is heat the soup. Please, go back in the lounge.'

'I enjoy helping you,' Lisette insisted, and met her mother's level glance with a faint smile. 'Together we can achieve twice as much in half the time.'

The three guests were family friends of long standing, and conversation flowed with the ease of familiarity.

Louise had excelled herself with a mouthwatering menu that brought genuine praise, although as far as Lisette was concerned she could have been forking sawdust into her mouth.

'My apologies, Maman,' she offered with quiet sincerity. 'I'm not in the least hungry.'

'Headache still there?' Jake queried with apparent concern, and it took considerable effort to retain her composure as he lifted a hand and touched gentle fingers to her temple. 'Perhaps we should forgo coffee so that I can get you home to bed, hmm?'

Lisette could almost hear a pin drop, and she momentarily closed her eyes in an effort to shut out the alert curiosity she knew to be evident in her mother's eyes. The instant they were alone, she would verbally *kill* him.

'*Chérie*, you should have told me,' Louise chastised gently. 'Have you taken anything for it?'

She forced a smile and effected a faint shrug. 'A few hours ago. Really, it's not that bad.' Rising to her feet, she began stacking plates ready to carry into the kitchen. 'I'll load the dishwasher while you set up for a game of cards.'

It helped to bury herself briefly in such a domestic task, although Louise's crockery and cutlery were dealt with more vigorously than usual. By comparison the crystal glassware was treated with exquisite care, and when she re-entered the lounge her features portrayed an outward serenity.

No one, she determined, would even guess at the depth of her anger. Except Jake, whose dark eyes held a gleam of mocking cynicism, and for an instant her own blazed with the strength of her antipathy, then she took a seat opposite him and watched as Louise began to deal the cards.

It was almost eleven when the game finished, and Lisette felt an unaccustomed tightening in her stomach as the evening came to a close.

'*Merci*, Maman,' she murmured as she kissed her mother goodnight, and in the car she simply sank back against the leather cushioning and stared sightlessly into space as Jake eased the vehicle down the driveway and on to the road.

'How *dare* you?' Lisette finally accused dully as the car picked up speed.

'Precisely what have I dared?' His drawl held chilling softness, and she caught the faint gleam of amusement in the slanted glance he cast her before the road claimed his attention.

Resentment flared deep inside, bubbling to the surface in choked rage. 'I hate you. *Hate*, do you understand?' Her hands clenched together with the force of her anger, and it was all she could do not to lash out at him.

'You'll only succeed in worsening your headache,' he indicated silkily.

'Don't patronise me, damn you!' Stupid angry tears clouded her vision, and she shook her head in silent antipathy to the man who seemed bent on her destruction.

'Juggling fast-moving traffic and a hysterical female at the same time aren't conducive to a safe journey,' Jake drawled. 'Either I stop the car and we have this out now, or you can save all that fine fury until we get home, where I can deal with it effectively. The choice is yours.'

'You're not going to *deal* with anything! Oh,' she berated in helpless rage, 'take me back to Frankston. I'll stay overnight with Louise.' Her eyes widened as he slowed down and eased the car to a halt on the side of the highway.

He doused the headlights and switched off the ignition, then he unclipped his seatbelt and turned towards her.

'*You*,' Lisette blazed, 'are the most arrogant, dictatorial man I've ever had the misfortune to meet! How Adam could be your father is a complete mystery.'

'The comparison obviously being that he was gullible, and I'm not?'

Her hand connected with a cracking slap to the side of his jaw, and in the ensuing silence she sat staring at him with angry, horrified eyes at the realisation of her action and its possible consequences.

For one totally wild moment she considered escaping from the car and flagging down a passing motorist, but even as her hand reached for the doorclasp strong fingers caught her arm in a painful grip.

'Have you considered you'll be in infinitely more danger out there than in here?' Jake demanded in a voice that sounded like steel slicing through silk.

Lisette attempted to wrench out of his grasp, and failed dismally. 'Let me go, damn you!'

With consummate ease he pulled her into his arms, and she twisted her head to one side as his mouth threatened to fasten on hers, except that he'd already anticipated such a reaction, and there could be no escape as he took possession in a kiss that was neither a punishment nor an appeasement, but simply a deliberate attempt to invade her senses.

She fought against him, physically and emotionally, in a determined effort not to be subjugated in any way. Except that she hadn't counted on the electric awareness that tingled through her veins then surged to encompass her whole being with such an intensity that she became lost, and in the end fought against herself and her own damnable reaction to his blatantly sexual onslaught.

It seemed an age before he relinquished her mouth, and she sank back in the seat feeling totally enervated. Her head throbbed with tension, and she lifted shaky fingers to her temple.

He was far too close, and her eyes widened nervously as he shaped her face with his hands, tilting it so that she had no choice but to meet his brooding gaze.

The pad of his thumb traced a gentle pattern over her lips, feeling their swollen contours tremble slightly beneath his touch, then she closed her eyes in self-defence as his lips brushed across her forehead before trailing down to rest at the edge of her mouth.

'Did you have to humiliate me by implying a mythical *affaire*?' Her eyes searching his were filled with pain.

'*Affaire* implies a degree of intimacy we have yet to achieve,' he gently mocked, and her chest constricted at the degree of purpose apparent in his words, the unspoken intention that it was merely a matter of where and when.

Without a further word he turned towards the wheel and re-started the engine, then he eased the car back on to the highway.

Lisette sat staring out beyond the windscreen at the quickly passing night-time scenery. Houses alive with light, others in total darkness. High walls, enveloping shrubbery casting dark shadows that appeared to double their size. The almost blinding light from oncoming headlights—light she instinctively shrank from as their probing beams left her feeling exposed and incredibly vulnerable.

There was no sense of the passage of time, and it was only when the Jaguar swooped down into the well-lit underground car park beneath the Toorak apartment block that she was able to focus on the fact they had arrived home.

She slid out from the passenger seat and moved towards the lift, aware that Jake walked at her side. Within minutes she'd reach the sanctuary of her apartment, and no matter how decadent it might appear she had every intention of sleeping in the following morning. The lift ascended, and transported them swiftly to her floor, and it wasn't until the doors closed behind her that she realised Jake had followed in her wake.

'I'm quite capable of unlocking my own door.'

'Then do it, Lisette,' he bade quietly, watching as she inserted the key.

'You're not coming in.' She heard the faint hint of desperation in her voice, and closed her eyes at her own stupidity. Jake, if he was determined, would do whatever he wanted, regardless of anything she said. 'Oh, for heaven's sake—don't you ever listen?'

'Take off your coat and sit down. I'll heat some milk.' His gaze was unyielding, and she flinched beneath his raking appraisal. 'Where do you keep the brandy?'

'I don't need hot milk and brandy, and I especially don't need you as a nursemaid!'

'You're behaving like a fractious child,' he drawled hatefully, and she closed her eyes in the hope that when she opened them again the room would be empty and Jake's image would merely be a figment of her imagination.

It didn't work. He moved closer—something that wasn't very good for her equilibrium.

'Just do as I say, hmm?'

'Is it just me? Or do you make a practice of asserting yourself with anyone who dares to defy you?'

'It's rarely necessary.'

She glimpsed the faint gleam of cynical humour in the depths of his eyes as he moved towards the kitchen, and she felt like flailing her fists against his broad back in sheer temper.

The apartment was warm, and with a pent-up sigh she shed her coat, then slipped out of her shoes. Her hands lifted automatically to her hair to loosen the pins holding the upswept style in place, then she padded restlessly round the lounge, touching an ornament, adjusting a picture-frame. Anything to ease the unbearable tension Jake seemed to generate.

Without thought she reached out and traced a finger over the carefree snapshot depicting herself and Adam on one of their many Sunday-afternoon picnics. The photograph had been taken before the ravages of his illness had become apparent, and he looked surprisingly fit. They were laughing, she with delight over the antics of a small puppy whose boundless energy combined with a natural tendency to show off had finally got the better of him, and Adam's eyes on her, his expression revealing such a wealth of indulgent affection that it brought a funny little catch to her throat every time she looked at the celluloid image.

Tears welled in her eyes, and she blinked to dispel them. He'd been such a sweet man, so considerate and caring. Special.

A slight sound alerted her attention and she looked up to see Jake standing a short distance away. His eyes were unfathomable as he extended a pottery mug. 'Your milk.'

Courtesy demanded that she thank him, and she uttered the appropriate words in a stilted tone, watching as he deposited the mug down on to a nearby table.

Somehow she expected him to leave, and when he moved to stand behind her she felt the painful thud of her heart as its beat increased in tempo.

'I'll see you out.'

'Not yet.'

She swung round to face him, her expression mirroring wary disbelief. 'It's late, I'm tired, and I have a headache. I'd like to go to bed.'

He reached out and cupped her face, and his faint smile held weary cynicism as she reared back from his touch as if from flame.

For a long time Jake just looked at her, almost as if he was attempting to define her soul, then, just as she thought she could bear his scrutiny no more, his hands moved to extract the loosened pins from her hair.

Every nerve-end stretched to its furthest limitation as his fingers began a gentle, tactile massage of her temples, seeking out the centre of pain, and after timeless seconds she closed her eyes, lost in the sensation he was able to evoke.

A relaxing head massage, that's all it is, she assured herself, and knew it to be a lie. It was a deliberate intrusion to the innermost region of her very existence. Invasive, pervasive and utterly destructive to her peace of mind.

If she had any common sense she'd move away, for he had the strangest effect on her equilibrium, making her aware of a primitive alchemy, a dramatic meshing of every one of her senses in a manner that was infinitely frightening.

It would be all too easy to lean back against him and invite his arms to slip down and curve about her waist. Her imagination was so vivid, she could almost *feel* his mouth against the hollow at the edge of her neck, and her breasts ached in anticipation of his touch, their peaks tightening in tell-tale recognition of a desire so acute that it was transcended only in an agony of self-denial.

What was the matter with her? She hardly needed to remind herself how much she hated him, surely?

Yet even as she thought to escape his fingers stilled and his hands fell away, leaving her with a terrible sense of loss.

'Has that made any difference?'

His drawled query jolted her back to reality, and she stepped quickly out of reach, loath to have him even guess at the state of her rampant emotions.

'Thank you.' Was that husky, indistinct voice her own? Heavens, she'd have to get a hold on herself! Without a further word she turned and walked towards the front door, only to find he had followed closely in her wake.

Her pulse-rate tripped and began a rapid erratic beat in recognition of his magnetic sensuality, and it was totally crazy but she became conscious of every breath she took, every beat of her heart.

'Sleep well, Lisette,' Jake taunted softly, bending his head low over hers, and she sensed rather than saw his faint smile an instant before his lips brushed across the fullness of her mouth.

Straightening, he moved past her and made his way towards the lifts, and she quickly closed the door behind him. Her lips tingled from his fleeting touch, and she walked slowly towards the kitchen. The mug of hot milk and brandy stood where Jake had placed it on the table, and she picked it up and sipped the contents slowly, grateful for their soothing effect.

When the mug was empty, she extinguished the lights and got ready for bed, slipping in between the warm covers to fall into a deep, dreamless sleep within minutes of her head touching the pillow.

CHAPTER SEVEN

LISETTE woke late, and after checking the time she rose and hastily showered, then pulled on designer jeans and a thick jumper. Louise was due to arrive for lunch en route to the airport to connect with her mid-afternoon flight to Sydney.

After a spartan breakfast of fruit Lisette spent the next hour restoring the apartment to its usual pristine order before sinking into a comfortable chair with a cup of coffee. The peal of the telephone was an unexpected intrusion, and her forehead creased as she crossed the room to pick up the extension.

'Have dinner with me tonight,' Jake's voice drawled down the line.

No conventional niceties, no identification. Just assumption that she must know who was calling, and worse, sheer audacity in expecting her to accept.

'I have other plans,' Lisette responded coolly.

He laughed, a soft, husky sound that sent shivers scudding down the length of her spine.

'Cancel them.'

'No.' Damn him, who did he think he was?

'Louise requested I keep an eye on you while she's away.'

Maman, how *dare* you? she agonised silently. 'No dinners, no lunches, and if you continue to invade my privacy I'll move into Louise's home for the

duration of her absence. And don't,' she added,
'simply arrive at my door. I'll refuse to let you in!'
The instant she finished speaking she depressed the
handset, then slowly replaced the receiver.

Anger unfurled from deep within and threatened
to consume her. Why, *how* had he managed to slip
beneath her skin when she'd been so determined
not to allow it?

Three weeks ago her life had seemed so uncomplicated, even serene. Her job, her private life had
developed a soothing predictability she felt infinitely comfortable with, and if occasionally she
pondered the absence of passion she inevitably dismissed it as something she could do without.

Jake's appearance had caused turmoil, making
her re-examine her priorities, even question her
inner self. And some of the answers weren't to her
liking.

Damn, she cursed shakily. Such introspection
only caused havoc with her nervous system. It was
infinitely preferable to keep her mind occupied,
rather than allow it the freedom to ponder the
vagaries of such a complex man as Jake
Hollingsworth.

The table was set, the soup heated and the bread
rolls warming in the oven when the intercom
buzzed, signalling Louise's arrival in the downstairs lobby, and within minutes Lisette was em-
bracing her mother in a warm hug at the door.

'Maman,' she breathed, welcoming her into the
lounge. 'How long do we have before we must leave
for the airport? Two hours?'

'Slightly less, *chérie*.'

'Then we'll eat straight away,' Lisette decided, as she took her mother's coat and folded it over the arm of a nearby chair.

'And you, Lisette,' Louise questioned with concern, 'the headache is all gone?'

'*Oui*, Maman.' Her smile was deliberately warm and guileless as she effected a faint shrug. 'A good night's sleep worked wonders.' No doubt induced by the generous measure of brandy Jake had added to the hot milk, she decided wryly.

Lunch was a convivial meal, over which they exchanged mutual news, discussed forthcoming social events, and there was no mention at all of Jake.

At the airport Lisette kissed her mother fondly as the flight was called, and as soon as Louise moved beyond the departure lounge Lisette turned and walked quickly out of the terminal to her car.

Feeling strangely restless, she drove towards the city instead of taking the more direct route to Toorak. There were notes she should study, letters to write, even the domestic chore of ironing, yet none held any appeal.

If she went home, there was always the possibility that Jake might take it upon himself to discover if her voiced intent to already have a date for the evening were fact or fiction.

After the briefest moment of indecision she opted to go to the movies—something she hadn't done on her own in ages. One of the girls in the typing pool at Andersen's had recommended a light romantic comedy that was currently receiving rave reviews, and Lisette felt light entertainment was exactly what she needed.

Parking wasn't difficult, and she entered the darkened cinema to take her seat just as the film began. Soon she became lost in the enchanting story, the excellent acting, and the empathy created by superb directorial ability and production. It all came together so beautifully that there was a sense of loss when the credits rolled against a backdrop of the closing scene.

There was a fast-food restaurant close by, and Lisette was tempted by the tantalising aroma to enter and place an order.

Seated, she ate with a sparing appetite that slowly diminished as she became increasingly aware of a group of young, outrageously attired teenagers who seemed bent on causing trouble. Not content with harassing a waitress, they turned their attention on to nearby fellow patrons, and just when Lisette thought the management would intervene the group rose noisily to their feet and shambled towards the entrance.

Lisette finished her meal, then sipped at the insipid-tasting coffee before discarding it. There was no reason for her to linger and, gathering up her bag, she slung the strap over one shoulder and prepared to leave.

It was dark outside, the sky inky black and oppressive with the threat of rain, and she stepped out briskly towards her car, her steps faltering fractionally as she turned the next corner and saw a group of four or five young people loitering within metres of her car.

Rather warily she kept walking, instinct warring with rationality as she carefully judged the distance. As she drew closer she was dismayed to recognise that they were the same teenagers who had made such a nuisance of themselves in the restaurant.

Pretend they're not there, she reassured herself silently. Another few seconds and you'll have reached the BMW, unlocked the door and be safely inside.

One chilling second later she knew she should have listened to her instincts. She heard loud voices, jeering, chanting obscenities, and although she had the key ready to insert into the lock they were already moving in to crowd her.

Rough hands caught at her bag, and she screamed out in the hope of attracting attention. Then she struggled, fear lending impetus to strength. Lunging out, she managed to inflict a few carefully learned self-defence body blows, but there were too many of them and the odds too great as she was pushed to the ground.

Lisette was aware of pain as she hit her head against something hard, then there was nothing.

A delicious floaty feeling invaded her body, an inner fragility that was clearly medically induced. Lisette could hear rustling movements, and firm fingers took hold of her wrist, held it, then let it go.

Strangely there was no sensation of pain, and for some reason she knew there should be. Slowly she opened her eyes, but the lids felt impossibly heavy, and it was simply easier to let them fall shut again.

At one stage she must have woken, for she was aware of bright light, the rumbling sound of voices, then she slowly surfaced into consciousness to find she was lying in a brightly lit room.

'Ah, you're awake,' a brisk feminine voice greeted her, and Lisette blinked as a warm, friendly face came into view. 'Do you remember anything of what happened?'

Did she? Memory surfaced slowly, kaleidoscopic sequences that all began to fit into place. 'Most of it. Until I passed out. Am I badly hurt?'

'A dislocated shoulder, two cracked ribs and bruising.' There was compassion evident as the woman's expression softened. 'Your husband is waiting outside. I'll send him in.'

Husband? She no longer had a husband! Lisette opened her mouth to say the words, but the nurse was already out the door, and the next instant Jake entered the room.

Lisette eyed him warily as he crossed round the bed to stand within touching distance. He looked, she decided, as if he was retaining rigid control, for there was a leashed quality about his stance that was vaguely intimidating, and his features resembled an inscrutable mask. Even his eyes were unfathomable, and she plucked at the bedcovers out of sheer nervousness.

'How are you feeling?'

She lifted her hand, then let it flutter down to the counterpane. 'I'm assured there are no breakages.'

'Have you any conception how foolish it is for a lone woman to park a car on an inner-city street after dark?'

She didn't need his tautly controlled anger. In fact, she didn't need him here at all!

'Spare me the recriminations, Jake.'

'Be grateful your driving-licence records you as Lisette LeClaire-Hollingsworth, with an address at the apartment building. When the police sought contact with a near relative, the manager immediately put the call through to me.'

She looked around the room, determining the exclusivity of the private suite. 'This isn't a public hospital.'

'No. I had you moved.' Cool, clipped words that held a degree of omnipotent power, and she shivered involuntarily.

'Louise?' Concern clouded her eyes, and she became agitated at the thought that her mother might already have been told. 'I don't want her to know—at least not yet. I'm not seriously hurt. She hasn't had a holiday in two years, and I refuse to worry her unnecessarily.'

'And if she rings the apartment and doesn't get an answer?'

'She'll assume I'm out. I left my answering machine on. Besides, I can put a call through to her in the morning.'

He examined her features, assessing the bright eyes and waxen pale cheeks with daunting scrutiny.

All of sudden she found his presence impossibly overpowering. There was an electric energy apparent that almost bordered on anger, and it was too much for her to cope with after the traumatic events of the early evening.

She closed her eyes against the sight of him, and she gave a faint start as she heard his husky imprecation.

'Go away, Jake,' she said wearily. 'You're giving me a headache.'

'Is there anything you need?'

She couldn't think of a thing she'd ask him to fetch, and she simply shook her head in silent negation.

He left without a further word, and she lay back against the nest of pillows looking impossibly fragile and wan, her petite frame swamped in its plain white hospital gown.

Within minutes the nurse bustled in, still faintly in awe of the man who had just vacated this suite. Three hours ago he'd had the place in an uproar, demanding the best specialist attention as the ambulance transferred this slip of a girl from a public hospital. Even calm, sensible Matron had quivered and given in to his every insistent demand.

With quiet capability she checked her patient and settled her for the night, administered an injection to dull the pain, then quietly left to continue her round.

When Lisette woke next it was morning, and the floaty feeling had gone. In its place was heavy dull pain—everywhere. It even hurt to breathe.

The doctor breezed into her suite just as she finished her breakfast, then again late afternoon, and her query regarding her length of stay was met with bland inscrutability.

'Mr Hollingsworth insists you shouldn't be discharged until tomorrow.'

'What do *you* think?' she persisted.

'I'd be prepared to release you now with certain stipulations.'

'Which are?'

'Don't attempt to use your arm for a week, and ensure you have adequate rest.'

'I'll arrange my own discharge,' Lisette said firmly.

'Mr Hollingsworth? Shouldn't he be informed?'

'I'll surprise him.'

'There are a few formalities. Sister will attend to them.'

Lisette didn't even make it out of her suite. In all probability she was never meant to, she decided darkly, as Jake appeared less than an hour later, looming impossibly tall in the confines of the room and assuming an imperturbable façade that didn't fool her in the slightest.

'What are you doing here?' Lisette spat, and incurred his level scrutiny.

'The doctor had the good sense to ring me. Something you obviously intended to neglect to do.' His voice sounded like velvet-encased steel, and there was no doubt of the anger beneath the surface of his control.

'I can take care of myself,' she countered with a touch of defiance, and his eyes swept her features in raking appraisal.

'In your present state, that's infinitely debatable.'

'You didn't have to collect me. I could have arranged a taxi.'

He thrust both hands into the pockets of his trousers in a controlled gesture, and his voice lowered to dangerous softness. 'Just how did you propose to pay the driver, Lisette? Your assailants got away with your bag and everything in it.'

The more mundane consequences of her attack came sharply into focus.

'My car——'

'Is safely secured in its reserved bay in the apartment underground car park,' Jake reassured smoothly. 'As there were no keys found, I've had a locksmith change the locks to the BMW and the apartment.' He paused, taking in the frailty of her appearance, and reined in his temper. 'If you're ready, we'll leave.'

They walked straight through Reception, and Lisette registered dimly that Jake must have taken care of her account. For some reason the thought irked her unbearably.

The Jaguar was parked immediately adjacent to the entrance, and he saw her safely seated before crossing round to slide in behind the wheel.

She didn't offer so much as a word during the short drive home, and she made only a token objection when he unlocked the door to her apartment and followed her inside.

'I'll fix you something to eat. And don't argue,' Jake cautioned silkily.

'I'm not hungry, and if you don't mind I'd like to be alone.'

'No, Lisette.'

Her eyes swept towards him, wide and impossibly angry. 'What do you mean—*no*?'

'You've discharged yourself from hospital ahead of time. Something the doctor would never have allowed had he known there was no one in residence to assist you.'

Her eyes widened into huge pools of incredulity as comprehension dawned. 'You can't mean to stay here,' she said at once.

'For the next few nights. Unless you acquaint Louise——'

'If I did, she'd board the next flight home. She *needs* this holiday, dammit! Besides, I'm perfectly fine, and there's absolutely nothing she can do by being here.'

'In that case, you'll have to put up with me,' Jake drawled, and a surge of anger rose to the surface.

'The hell I will!' Inwardly she felt like screaming with vexation. 'I can manage on my own!'

If he could have shaken her within an inch of her life, he would have. It was there in his eyes, the tightly leashed control in his stance, and she suppressed an involuntary shiver at the inadvisability of opposing him.

'Prove it.'

She looked at him, then glanced away, her chin tilting slightly in silent defiance.

'You only have the use of one arm, one hand. Try preparing a meal, or at the very least opening a can of food. I seriously doubt,' he continued with mocking cynicism, 'if you can manage to undress yourself.'

Her eyes flashed with indignant mutiny. 'All hell will freeze over before I'll allow you to take on that task!'

'Go make yourself something to eat, Lisette. Then get out of those clothes.'

She'd do it, even if the resultant pain killed her, she determined, moving past him, and in the kitchen she extracted bread, butter, a few eggs, some cheese. Then she took out a pan and heated it, broke the eggs into a cup and managed to whisk them.

Five minutes later she had a passable omelette, some toast, and coffee was percolating on the hotplate.

Her shoulder throbbed, and her ribs felt as if they were going to break every time she drew breath, but she was damned if she'd allow Jake to perceive any hint of her pain.

He watched her as a hawk eyed a dove, all keenly alert and waiting for the merest sign she might falter.

'Now go and get undressed.'

Without a word she made her way to the bedroom and closed the door. The jeans weren't too difficult, although her teeth were tightly clenched against the increasing pain as she struggled to shed the figure-hugging denim. Next came her knitted jumper and, no matter how she twisted and turned or manoeuvred, it was impossible to free herself of it.

A faint knock at the door froze her into immobility, and she raised large eyes stricken with futility and pain as Jake entered the room.

For one infinitesimal second his eyes blazed with ruthless intensity, then without a word he crossed to her side. With incredible gentleness he freed first one arm, then the other, and slipped the jumper over her head. Then he unclipped her bra and removed it, and she tensed, supremely conscious of the scanty silk and lace briefs that were all she had left to protect her from total nudity. She'd caught sight of several dark purplish bruises on her ribs via mirrored reflection this morning and been shocked.

Now she stood still as Jake's gaze travelled over each and every one of them. She didn't utter a word as he caught up her nightgown and carefully eased it over her head.

'Get into bed. I'll make a hot drink and bring it to you, together with the prescribed pain-killers.' His voice was authoritatively quiet, and she doubted if she had the energy to disobey him.

Slipping in between the sheets to lie against the pillows, everything hurt, even her hip where she'd fallen to the ground, her head ached, and all she wanted to do was close her eyes and not wake up for days.

It could have been a few minutes or ten when she felt the side of the bed depress, and her eyes slowly flickered open, their expression intensely vulnerable as she took the tablets from his outstretched hand.

Jake held the rim of the mug to her lips, and she sipped the warm contents slowly to wash first one then the other tablet down.

When the milk was finished he rose to his feet and subjected her to a level glance. 'If you need anything, just call.'

Lisette looked at him for a few timeless minutes, aware of the quiet forcefulness beneath his rugged exterior. It would be pointless to argue, and she didn't even try.

Instead she simply blocked him from her vision by veiling her eyes, and she unconsciously held her breath as he stood for several long seconds before he turned and left the room.

At some stage through the night she came sharply awake, unsure whether she'd cried out in her sleep. Then she did cry out as the bedside lamp sprang on, immediately bathing the room with a subdued golden glow. For one brief second she was locked into mesmeric fear, the memories of the previous night so incredibly vivid that their very clarity over-shadowed her vision. A husky oath lashed her sensitive ears, and she actively flinched as Jake sank down on to the bed and leaned towards her.

'I should bundle you into the car and re-admit you into hospital,' he uttered savagely.

'Because I had a nightmare?'

'Because,' he corrected bleakly, 'you're a stubborn, self-willed scrap of femininity who hasn't the good sense to recognise her own fallibility.'

'I don't want to go back to hospital.'

'Are you going to be sensible about accepting my help?' His eyes bored hers, inexorable and without mercy as he reiterated with dangerous softness, 'Don't deny you need it.'

'You must know I don't want you here,' she threw, sorely tried, and glimpsed the edge of his mouth twist in humourless cynicism.

'In this apartment?' he slanted. 'Or just your bedroom?'

'Both!'

The thought of having him here was almost more than she could bear, and his expression hardened fractionally.

'We'll discuss it in the morning.' He adjusted the dimmer-switch on her bedside lamp to low, then settled himself into a chintz-covered recliner chair a few feet distant.

Lisette looked at him with wide incredulous eyes. 'You can't mean to stay in my bedroom!'

'I've been here all the time,' he informed her drily.

She felt consumed with helpless rage at the hand fate had played. 'This is ridiculous.'

'Go to sleep, Lisette,' he drawled, and after what seemed an interminable length of time her lashes slowly fluttered down as she drifted into blissful sleep.

CHAPTER EIGHT

IN THE morning Lisette woke to the tantalising aroma of freshly brewed coffee and, inching carefully out of bed, she gathered up fresh underwear, a comfortable tracksuit with a zipped jacket, before entering the adjoining en suite bathroom.

Her hair posed a slight problem, but she managed to push its length into a shower-cap before stepping into the shower cubicle. Hot water cascaded over her body, refreshingly soothing, and afterwards she took time to complete her toilet. Attempting to fasten the clips on her bra proved to be a frustrating experience, and after several fruitless attempts she abandoned the scrap of silk and lace entirely.

It was amazing what you could achieve with only one hand, she decided, and equally remarkable how frustrating it could be without aid of the other!

With the jacket zipped to her throat, she slipped the sling over her neck and carefully adjusted it to accommodate the weight of her arm.

Jake displaying competence in the kitchen wasn't an image she'd previously envisaged, and her heart began a deep thudding beat at the sight of him deftly turning bacon and tomatoes in a skillet.

Fresh from a recent shower, he looked incredibly male, his dark towelling robe lending a rakish air she found infinitely disturbing. He turned and directed her a long, level look from cool grey eyes that were sweepingly analytical in their appraisal before lightening somewhat as his mouth curved into a warm smile.

Lisette curbed the instinct to smile back. The memory of last night's high-handedness was still too fresh in her mind to negate any harboured resentment.

He didn't look, she brooded, as if he'd spent most of the night sleeping in a recliner chair, for the length of his frame would have precluded even minimum comfort.

'Good morning.'

His drawling voice gave her goose-bumps in the most unlikely places, and she returned his greeting as she extracted a glass from a nearby cupboard and crossed to the refrigerator.

'Sit down. This will be ready in a minute.'

'I never eat a cooked breakfast,' she told him. Orange juice, muesli with skimmed milk and a chopped banana, followed by coffee was her usual fare.

'Then tell me what you have, and I'll make it.'

Lisette took out the bottle of orange juice and poured some into a glass. 'At least let me determine my limitations,' she declared, closing the refrigerator door.

'Still determined to be fiercely independent?' Jake queried silkily, and she suppressed a slight shiver. She finished her orange juice and apportioned muesli into a dish with a hand that shook. Be positive, she admonished silently.

'I can manage on my own.'

'So far you haven't managed a convincing display.'

The nerves in her stomach activated themselves and twisted into a painful knot, pulling cruelly as her emotions began to shred.

'Last night you said we'd discuss your expressed need to be here.'

'By all means, let's have a discussion,' Jake declared with thinly veiled mockery, and his cynicism struck an antagonistic chord.

'Don't patronise me,' she said fiercely.

'In half an hour I'll be out of this apartment,' he stated in a deadly soft voice. 'I've put some soup I found in the refrigerator into a bowl, ready for you to heat in the microwave for lunch. My mobile phone number is written down, and I'll prepare dinner when I get in—around five.' His eyes lanced right through to her soul. 'Accept you have no choice, Lisette. To fight against me is futile and merely a waste of energy.'

She wanted to hit him, to lash out verbally at his ruthless determination, and her mouth trembled with reaction. He aroused feelings she'd never known she possessed, and if she stayed in this room a second longer she'd never be able to restrain herself.

Without a word she simply walked away from him to shut herself in her bedroom, where she remained until he left.

Within minutes of re-entering the kitchen she sat down at the table and browsed idly through the morning's newspaper while she finished her breakfast.

The day loomed long, and after viewing a documentary on television she slotted in a video. At eleven the intercom buzzed, and she crossed to activate the audio-visual monitor.

A delivery boy in uniform carrying an elegant bouquet of flowers came into view, and she instructed him to deposit the floral tribute at Reception.

Ten minutes later the receptionist rang her doorbell, presented the flowers, made genuine enquiries as to her health, then returned to the elevator.

The card expressed the good wishes from all the staff at Andersen's, and she found a vase, filled it, and spent time carefully arranging the beautiful blooms.

After lunch she felt tired, and opted to rest for an hour, sleeping much longer than she intended, for it was after three when she woke. A cup of coffee would help clear her head, she determined, and the percolator was almost ready when the intercom buzzed.

More flowers, she mused as she activated the monitor. Although this time the delivery boy was hidden from view.

'Leave them with Reception, and they'll arrange for their delivery,' Lisette instructed, wondering who else could possibly be sending her flowers. Apart from the staff at Andersen's, the only person who knew of her accident was Jake.

'We've been requested to deliver them personally.'

Her forehead creased with momentary perplexion, then a latent sixth sense reared its cautionary head. Only the top of the delivery boy's head was visible, for the manner in which he was holding the flowers completely obliterated his features.

'For security reasons, all deliveries must be left with Reception.'

With strange fascination she watched as the flowers lowered to reveal the boy's identity, and shock rippled through her body as she recognised him as one of the group of five who had participated in her assault.

He didn't say a further word, and she watched as he deposited the flowers down on to the ground before turning and walking away. The nerves inside her stomach tightened, and she pondered whether she should report the incident or not.

The insistent knock on the door caused her to start with nervous apprehension, and she stood transfixed for several seconds before crossing the lounge. As a precautionary measure she slid the security chain into position.

'Lisette?'

Jake! Relief washed through her, and she immediately released the chain and opened the door. 'I wasn't expecting you this early.'

'The meeting finished ahead of time.' Grey eyes raked her pale features with a faintly narrowed gaze as he entered the room. 'You're as nervous as a kitten.'

Oh, lord, should she tell him? 'A fairly natural reaction, wouldn't you say?' she managed quietly.

'If that's all it is.' He moved into the lounge, deposited a large shopping bag on to a nearby chair, then turned to regard her with studied care.

'Why don't you have a drink?' She had to say something, otherwise she'd wilt beneath his compelling scrutiny.

'Soon,' Jake dismissed. 'How was your day?'

'The staff at Andersen's sent flowers.' Her eyes dilated and became faintly luminous. 'I rested a while, then watched television.'

Heavens, they sounded like a comfortable married couple, she decided a trifle hysterically. Except *comfortable* was the last adjective she'd accord in relation to Jake Hollingsworth.

Unbidden, an image rose to taunt her—an image that was infinitely devilish and totally insane.

As much as she assured herself she hated him, she was unable to dispel an intrinsic, almost elemental fascination for the man standing a few feet distant. She could almost *feel* the magnetic pull of his powerful masculinity, and her body trembled as a slow warmth coursed through her veins, bringing alive a multitude of sensations she was loath to analyse.

It would be wonderful to seek the comfort of his arms, to relay her fears and receive his reassurance. Yet such a course was madness, and she sensed rather than heard his swift intake of breath, then he was standing far too close, and there was nothing she could do to prevent the firm pressure of his thumb and forefinger as he caught hold of her chin and lifted it.

'Don't be a heroine, Lisette.' His eyes lanced through the defensive barrier she'd erected with relentless determination. 'The louts who attacked you have your bag, which accesses your identification and address.' His fingertips traced the outline of her mouth with feather-lightness, then slid to cup her face. 'If any attempt at contact has been made, I want to know about it.'

Indecision momentarily clouded her features, and a slight shiver raked her slender frame. In a halting voice she told him what had happened, and when she finished he released her and crossed to the phone.

As soon as that call was concluded he reached for her private line and punched out a series of digits, then spoke quietly into the receiver.

The police, Lisette deduced, overhearing the concise ruthlessness in his voice, and she turned towards the lounge, crossing to the large expanse of glass with its magnificent far-reaching view towards tall city buildings in one direction and suburbia in the other.

With a sense of brooding introspection she reflected that none of this would have happened if she hadn't attempted to avoid Jake's dinner invitation by inventing plans she didn't have and then subsequently feeling obliged to manufacture a reason for being absent from her apartment for several hours.

Fear had never been her companion, and she hated Jake, and *herself*, for an inadvertent action that had brought such a distressing aftermath.

It seemed an age before he rejoined her, and she cast his strongly etched features an enquiring glance.

'Reception noticed the flowers left at the main entrance, and they brought them in only to find there was no accompanying card. The security monitor is being checked now for a photographic record of his identity. They'll ring when it's available, and then it will be a simple matter for you to confirm an identification. The police will take it from there.'

Her fingers moved restlessly against the crest of a nearby chair. 'I don't suppose it's possible he might have had an attack of conscience, and the flowers were meant as a token apology?'

He viewed her thoughtfully. 'Why no card? Even the shortest message would have sufficed.'

Lisette affected a faint shrug. 'Maybe he got cold feet, or suspected the existence of a surveillance camera.' They could rationalise any number of possibilities and still come to an inaccurate conclusion. The very worst scenario involving intimidation and further assault in a bid to ensure her silence was left unvoiced.

'Have you contacted Louise?'

'Yes. This morning.' Lisette started visibly as his hand covered hers and stilled the restless tracing pattern of her fingers atop the chair. Startled, she snatched her hand away, hating herself for the effect he had on her emotions.

Contrarily, she wanted to be alone and assume her familiar orderly existence. Yet his presence, while infinitely disturbing to her peace of mind, lent a reassuring protection she was loath to discard.

'I'll organise dinner.' His voice held a tinge of cynical humour, and she met his gaze fearlessly, aware that his strong masculine features were sculpted by a well-defined bone-structure that portrayed a harsh indomitability.

'I'm not very hungry.'

She watched as he shrugged off his suit jacket and hung it over the back of chair, then he removed cufflinks and deftly turned back his shirtsleeves.

His forearms were liberally sprinkled with dark springy hair, and well-corded with developed muscle and sinew.

'Come and tell me where everything is kept.'

Curiosity finally won out as she followed him into the kitchen. 'What do you intend cooking?'

Jake shot her a musing glance. 'Something relatively simple. Steak, vegetables. Heating an apple pie the delicatessen assured me was home-made.'

A hidden gleam of amusement lightened her eyes, and her mouth curved to form a faint smile. 'Home-made apple pie sounds typically American. I don't imagine you cook very often?'

His shoulders moved in an imperceptible shrug as he began unpacking the shopping bag. 'A lot of business deals are cemented over a social meal.'

'Not to mention all those intimate dinners with your current . . .' she paused slightly to give delicate emphasis '. . . companion.'

'Lover,' he substituted with lazy tolerance, and she found herself held captive by a pair of riveting grey eyes.

Inside she was a trembling mass of nerves. Imagining that lithe, powerful frame engaged in the sexual act and the degree of his passionate involvement sent her emotions spiralling into a state of frenzied confusion.

'I'm sure Melanie is suitably appreciative.'

'Whatever Melanie's aspirations,' Jake drawled, 'she hasn't made it into my bed.'

'Not for the want of trying.' The voiced observation slipped out without thought, and his eyes speared hers with a degree of faint mockery.

'A man prefers to be the hunter.'

Is that what you're doing to me? she longed to scream at him. 'The thrill of the chase, followed by the satisfaction of the kill,' Lisette substituted, holding his gaze with determined bravado. 'And afterwards the male of the species walks away, having achieved his objective.'

'Without thought for his prey?'

Somehow this verbal thrust and parry had digressed on to the shaky ground of *double entendre*, and Lisette was no match for his skilled exchange.

'I'll set the table,' she essayed stoically, and turned away, determined not to allow him licence to see into her soul.

The meal was superb, and they had barely finished eating when the intercom buzzed, identifying a representative of the police force requesting an interview.

After an hour of intensive questions and photographic identification, the policeman finally left, and, although he had no definite lead, he was confident it was only a matter of time. Meanwhile, he advised extra care with security measures.

Lisette began collecting plates from the table and transferring them on to the sink, all too aware of Jake's proximity as he cleaned pots and pans in hot, sudsy water.

When the task was finished he dried his hands, then caught up his jacket and hooked it over one shoulder. 'I won't be long. I need to collect a change of clothes from my apartment.'

Something twisted painfully inside her stomach. 'There's no need for you to stay tonight. I'll be fine on my own.'

His gaze trapped hers, and she felt every single hair on her body prickle with inexplicable foreboding. 'We settled the necessity for someone to stay with you in the apartment.'

'*You* settled it,' she cried wretchedly.

'Until the police have some conclusive lead, I don't consider it wise for you to be alone.'

'I'm tired of being subjugated to what you want!'

'Don't even think of locking me out, Lisette,' he said hardly as he walked towards the front door. 'If you do, I can promise you'll curse the day you were born.'

Anger surged up inside her, venting itself in inexplicable rage. 'What *is* it with you?' Her breath came out in short gasps as the pain from her ribs almost robbed her of the power of speech. 'This is *my* apartment, *my* life, and you have no part in either!'

He reached the door, opened it, then closed it quietly behind him. Somehow his control was the last straw, and she followed him, then slid the safety-chain in place.

He was a force unto himself—invincible, compelling, *lethal*.

For all of three minutes she was caught up with the resolve to leave the chain in place, and to hell with the consequences. Except common sense won out, and when he returned she deliberately waited a few seconds before crossing to open the door.

'This is totally ridiculous,' Lisette muttered as Jake moved into the lounge.

She was so incredibly angry, with herself for being in such an impossibly invidious position, and with him, for his stubborn, autocratic insistence in playing the role of her protector.

'Give it a break, Lisette,' Jake directed hardily. 'You're beginning to sound like a needle stuck in a groove.'

She rounded on him at once, hating his implacability. 'If it weren't for *you*, I wouldn't be in this position.' She paused and thoughtlessly drew breath, only to wince at the immediate pain.

'You think I'm not aware of that?'

His silky query sent a *frisson* of fear slithering across the surface of her skin, and she stood perfectly still beneath his dark, indomitable gaze.

She wanted to physically hit out at him, to verbally castigate him for everything he represented. Her eyes warred silently with his, their dark golden-green depths alive with a latent anger so intense that she felt like a volcano in danger of erupting.

The sudden peal of the telephone sounded loud in the electric tension generated in the room, and she moved quickly to answer it.

'Lisette? How are you? I rang the office late this afternoon only to be told you were absent on sick leave. Are you OK?'

'Alex—I'm fine.' It was a downright lie, of course. Her physical health left something to be desired, and her emotions were in a state of utter chaos.

'Would you like a visitor for an hour?'

She was about to say no, except a tiny imp silently taunted, Why not? She wasn't sick, only mildly incapacitated. Besides, she possessed a strong desire to ruffle Jake's composure. Alex's presence in her apartment would prove a welcome diversion.

'What time?'

'Twenty minutes?'

'See you soon.'

She replaced the receiver and turned to discover that she was the object of Jake's veiled scrutiny. Her eyes assumed a fiery sparkle, and her chin lifted in a gesture of defiance.

'Xenides?' he queried with dangerous silkiness, and she spluttered into furiously angry speech.

'Is there any reason why Alex shouldn't visit?'

There was a glimmer of wry amusement apparent in those grey eyes that made her seethe with silent anger.

'Did I imply there was?'

If she didn't escape from this room *now*, she'd say something infinitely regrettable! 'I'm going to freshen up.'

Lisette entered her bedroom and carefully closed the door. The temptation to slam it was almost irresistible, but she managed to restrain it—just.

Her tracksuit would have to remain, she decided a trifle grimly, unless she solicited Jake's assistance in helping her change, and she was *damned* if she'd do that!

After several attempts endeavouring to pin up her hair, she simply gave up trying and subjected its length to a vigorous brushing. She emerged into the lounge to hear the deep burr of the intercom, and she glanced quickly towards Jake, who merely slanted one eyebrow in musing silence.

Alex's features portrayed suitable concern in the security monitor, and minutes later that concern was volubly verbalised as he entered the apartment.

'Alex. How are you?' The slight American inflexion lent emphasis to the deep, drawling tones as Jake rose to his feet from the depth of the cushioned armchair, and Lisette glimpsed the almost comical expression of disbelief on Alex's features before it was carefully masked.

'Come and sit down,' Jake bade with the urbanity of long association. 'Will you have some coffee? I was about to make some.'

How dared he make a social occasion of Alex's visit, and how *dared* he give the impression he had every right to be in her apartment? Lisette seethed.

'I'll make it,' she said quickly in an effort to establish some sort of territorial claim.

'Nonsense, *chérie*,' Jake discounted gently. 'Sit down and entertain your guest. It won't take me long.'

Chérie? What the hell was he playing at?

'What happened? Were you involved in an accident?' Alex queried, indicating the sling supporting her shoulder.

She had just finished telling him, discounting it as of little consequence, when Jake entered the lounge carrying a tray laden with her best china, a plate of sliced home-made cake, as well as sugar and cream.

Depositing it down on to the coffee-table, he played host with the ease of long practice, then sank back into the chair he'd previously occupied and gave every indication of joining their conversation.

Lisette retained no clear memory of anything that passed between the three of them under the guise of spontaneous chit-chat, neither could she determine the length of Alex's visit. All she was aware of was Jake very skilfully painting a credible picture of himself in the role of her benefactor and protector. Not only that, he deliberately implied that he had taken up temporary residence in her apartment.

By the time Alex left, Lisette was so furiously angry that she could scarcely contain herself, and in a bid for control she began stacking cups and saucers together on to the tray.

'Go to bed,' Jake drawled. 'I'll take care of those.'

'You've already done enough!'

One eyebrow rose in silent query, and the faint mocking gleam in those cool grey eyes was sufficient to tip her over the edge into volcanic rage.

Without thought she picked up a cup and threw it at him, uncaring whether it reached its target or not. The sheer act of throwing it released some of her pent-up fury, and she watched with a sense of detached fascination as he caught the cup in one hand, then slowly, carefully, placed it down on to a nearby table.

The very structured movement of his actions should have alerted her, and her eyes widened in open defiance as he closed the distance between them.

'Don't you dare touch me!'

He was so close that she could sense the warmth of his body, discern the faint exclusive tones of his aftershave.

'Oh, I *dare*, Lisette,' he drawled softly, and his eyes resembled sheer shards of obsidian slate. 'And my touch will be so incredibly restrained, you won't feel any pain.' His hands lifted to frame her face, and his head slowly lowered down to hers. 'Although afterwards, you may very well wish you had.'

Her lips parted instinctively, silently imploring him to desist. Except it was far too late, and she stood in horrified silence as his thumbs traced the delicate structure of her cheekbones before slipping down to rest at each corner of her mouth.

Slowly, and with infinite care, he probed the soft curve of her lower lip, smiling faintly as he felt it tremble, and his eyes flared as the tip of her tongue darted out in a gesture of involuntary nervousness. His mouth moved to cover hers, teasing with such evocative sensitivity that it was all she could do not to moan an entreaty for him to deepen the kiss.

Except he didn't, and instead he conducted a calculated assault that sought to destroy her defences, coaxing, cajoling in such a manner that gave licence to the degree of his sensual expertise.

He filled her senses, and made her ache for more. Yet beneath the gentleness was the hidden threat of steel—the promise of an erotic possession so fraught with emotion that its onslaught could only prove a pillaging, plundering invasion that would bring tumultuous devastation in its wake.

An inner voice screamed in agonised rejection, and Lisette felt cold, so cold that she began to shake. Huge tears welled, blurring her vision, then spilled to roll in slow rivulets down each cheek.

It was a deliberate rape of her senses, a parody that was meant to teach her a lesson. Pride forbade she beseech him to stop, and she stood there, captured by the silent strength of him as he annihilated her pride, her very soul.

She was dying inside, she decided dully as at last he lifted his head, and she lowered her lashes in protective self-defence against that hard, encompassing grey gaze as he raked her features. Caught up in the ravages of her emotions, she swayed slightly, then cried out as he placed an arm beneath her knees and swept her high against his chest.

The distance to the bedroom seemed incredibly long, and she could only look at him as he lowered her to stand close to the bed's edge.

With extreme care he removed the sling, then slid the zip fastening the edges of her tracksuit-top down to the waist before carefully freeing one sleeve, then the other.

Mesmerised by the depth and intensity of his gaze, she crossed her arms in a protective gesture, then cried out as his hands caught hold of her wrists and carefully lowered them to each side of her waist. Her bruises had lost none of their vivid purplish tinge, and her eyes widened and became glittery with anger.

With studied ease he released one of her hands, then he trailed his fingers across her breasts, deliberately brushing their tender peaks before cupping the burgeoning fullness of one then moving to caress the other in an action that brought a rush of telltale colour to her cheeks.

'Don't.' The single negation came out as a tortured whisper, and she momentarily closed her eyes against the slight cynical twist of his mouth as it curved in acceptance of his effect on her body.

Jake's hands slid to her waist, and her eyes darkened with fearful apprehension as he slipped the tracksuit bottoms down over her hips and let them fall to the floor.

Not content, he traced the line of her bikini briefs with an idle forefinger, and she reared back, her stomach tautening against his touch.

'Please—don't,' she beseeched, then she cried out as his fingers brushed across the silken V that arrowed between her thighs. '*Jake*!'

Slowly his hand trailed to the indentation of her navel, savouring the softness of her skin as he traced an evocative path to her throat.

'Be grateful for your injuries.' His voice was a soft drawl, and dark eyes lanced hers, narrowing faintly as he glimpsed the defensiveness apparent in their depths. 'If it weren't for them, I'd take you all the way to hell before permitting you a taste of heaven.' His fingers captured her chin, and his thumb parted the trembling softness of her mouth.

Lisette was conscious of the pulse at the base of her throat thudding impossibly loud in a quickened beat, and when he released her she actually thought she might fall.

Seconds later he caught up her nightgown and slipped it over her head.

'Now get into bed, and sleep. If you can.'

In a daze she turned and slid in between the sheets to lie staring at the ceiling long after he'd left the room.

During the following few days Lisette resigned herself to being the perfect patient, and she was so sweetly tractable in her bid to provide Jake with no reason to issue the mildest chastisement for any of her actions that she surprised even herself.

The police tracked down her assailants, and subsequent investigations proved none of the five apprehended held any previous convictions. Extensive questioning revealed that the flowers delivered to her apartment building *had* been intended as an act of apologetic atonement, and she elected not to press charges on their parents' undertaking that parental discipline would be enforced.

A medical examination on Friday elicited professional clearance to resume work on Monday, and Jake, although he continued to insist on sharing her evening meal every night, assumed the indolent persona of an affectionate friend.

Although there was a watchfulness apparent beneath the smiling façade, and Lisette wasn't able to shake off the feeling that he was merely biding his time.

CHAPTER NINE

LOUISE was suitably upset on her return to learn what had transpired during her absence, and alternately chastised Lisette for keeping her in ignorance and lauded Jake for his kindness.

Lisette downplayed the entire event, preferring to put it to the furthest reaches of her mind.

Work acted as a panacea. That and the fact Jake spent much of his time during the following few days jetting between Sydney, the Gold Coast, Cairns and Perth. In his absence she dealt with Hank Preston on a business level and spent time with Louise.

Consequently it came as a delightful surprise on Wednesday when Alex rang her at the office and invited her to join him and a group of friends at the theatre that evening.

'*Les Misérables*,' Alex enlightened, and received her enthusiastic response. 'I'll collect you at six-thirty, and we'll get something to eat first. OK?'

Lisette agreed at once, and replaced the receiver with a smile. Alex was amusing company, and it would do her good to go out.

She was almost ready when the phone rang, and she quickly snatched up the receiver.

'Lisette.' Jake's deep faintly accented drawl came down the line, and she felt the familiar clutch of nervous tension begin in the region of her stomach.

'Is this a social call? I'm just on my way out.'

'In that case, I won't keep you. Enjoy yourself, *ma petite*.'

That did it. 'I'm not your—*petite*,' she responded furiously. 'And you can stop being so darned condescending!'

'Anything else you'd care to fling at me?'

Oh, he was *impossible*! 'Why don't you ring Melanie? She'll be delighted to talk to you for as long as you choose.'

His husky laughter was the living end, and she felt a rush of colour flood her cheeks as he continued quietly in very good French to explain why he thought she was angry and what he planned to do about it.

'You——' Words momentarily failed her, and it gave her great satisfaction to lapse into an expressive volley of rapid French in a bid to tell him precisely what she thought of him, then she replaced the receiver before he had the opportunity to respond.

She should have experienced a sense of satisfaction at succeeding in some small measure against him. Instead, there was recognition that one minor victory did not constitute a battle won.

The stage production was excellent, and in a determined bid to dispel Jake's image she agreed to go on to a nightclub with Alex and his friends. The music was too loud, added to which was the crush of too many patrons, and after an hour she decided she'd had enough.

'I'll order a taxi,' Lisette indicated close to Alex's ear, and he shook his head.

'No. I'll take you. I have the feeling that Jake Hollingsworth would cause me to suffer grievous bodily harm if anything happened while you were in my care.'

'You're being fanciful,' Lisette opined, and caught his wry expression.

'No, dear girl. I can assure you I'm not.'

It was after midnight when Alex drew the car to a halt outside the apartment entrance and safely inside she crossed to summon a lift.

Within minutes it transported her to the seventh floor, and she entered her apartment, then came to an abrupt halt at the sight of Jake standing perfectly at ease close to the wide expanse of glass overlooking the street.

'What are you doing here?' Lisette demanded in scandalised query. 'And how did you get in?'

The unexpected sight of him threw her way off balance, and just looking at him made her frighteningly aware that the chemistry between them combined in a volatile, combustible force.

'With one of two spare keys the locksmith handed me when he changed the lock on your apartment door.'

Her eyes glittered with brilliant fire as she fought against indignant anger and lost. 'You had no right——'

'Spare me the recriminations, Lisette.' He lifted a hand and raked impatient fingers through his hair. 'I've had a rough day, and an even rougher flight from Sydney.'

'So why are you here?'

His mouth curved to form a cynical smile. 'Would you believe—to see you?'

For the space of several long seconds she was robbed of the power of speech, and then there wasn't one logical word she could summon to mind that would qualify as an adequate response.

'At least Xenides had the good sense to personally ensure you reached home.'

'Alex is a friend. I enjoy his company.'

One eyebrow slanted in a mocking gesture. 'Are you telling me you don't enjoy mine?'

Dear lord, how did she answer that? With considerable care, an inner voice cautioned. Yet even as she searched for the appropriate answer he continued with dangerous softness, 'If you want to engage in a mad social whirl, I'm prepared to indulge you.'

'Why?' Lisette demanded baldly.

He moved towards hers, halting to stand within touching distance, then he lifted a hand and brushed the tips of his fingers across her cheek. 'Don't play games, Lisette,' he warned softly.

Angry resentment unfurled deep within and lent her eyes a dark fiery sparkle. 'You're the one who's playing games!'

His hand slid to cup her chin, tilting it so that she had no choice but to look at him. 'I don't like to think of you in the company of other men.'

It was an unexpected admission, and she was conscious of an elevated nervous tension, a heightened awareness that was almost frightening, and she forced herself to meet his gaze with fearless disregard. 'You have no right to make that kind of statement.'

Just a glance at the sensual curve of his mouth was enough to set her pulse racing, and she became prey to an entire gamut of emotions, none of which was enviable.

He continued as if she hadn't spoken. 'Tell me how it was between you and my father.'

A painful hand clutched her heart, and she stood immobile, her eyes becoming wide and faintly stricken. Oh, heavens, where did she start? And should she even begin?

She looked at him carefully, seeing the strength etched on his ruggedly attractive features, the dark, brooding intensity evident in his steel-grey eyes, and she unconsciously drew in a deep breath.

'You know how I met Adam.'

His eyes seemed incredibly dark, and his mouth assumed a stark cruelty that made her feel terribly afraid.

'I need to hear it.'

Three years ago she'd wanted to explain, but he had refused to listen. Now, it was more difficult than she'd ever imagined, and she consciously sought her words with care.

'Adam dined frequently at the restaurant where I was waitressing most nights to help finance my way through university,' she began quietly, holding his gaze without any difficulty at all. 'We became friends.'

Jake didn't say a word. He just stood, waiting for her to continue, and after a few seemingly long seconds she forced herself to carry on.

'A friendship which had little to do with chronological age. He was a very caring man. Kind, thoughtful. I enjoyed his company very much.' Her eyes were clear and steady, their gaze remarkably direct. 'When Adam asked me to marry him, I presented every logical reason to refuse.'

'He obviously managed to convince you.'

'He didn't want to be alone,' Lisette said simply.

'Dammit,' he swore huskily, 'you were out all day, and surely had to study every night?'

Her chin lifted fractionally. 'He rested while I was at university, and we spent the evenings together. Talking, enjoying selected television programmes until he became tired. Then I would retrieve my textbooks and work on my assignments.'

'Quality time,' Jake mocked, and in that moment she hated him.

'Adam thought so.'

'And bed, Lisette?' he queried cynically. 'Did your generosity extend to pleasing him there?'

She held his gaze steadily, her eyes wide with unflinching solemnity. 'That's none of your business.'

'Isn't it?' Jake emanated brooding savagery from every nerve and fibre. '*Isn't it*?' His hands caught hers in a crushing grip, and she cried out with pain.

'For three years I've been eaten up with varying degrees of rage,' he revealed hardly. 'All of it centred around *you*.' His eyes speared hers, lancing right through to her soul. 'I couldn't comprehend your presence in my father's life, much less condone the marriage.' Not for the first time, if he could have shaken her within an inch of her life, he would have. The silent threat was evident beneath the rigid extent of his control.

'At first I was sure it had to be his money,' he continued ruthlessly. 'Yet you didn't appear to encourage him to spend any. I kept waiting for the punchline, but it never came. No matter which pigeon-hole I attempted to place you in, not one of them seemed to fit.' For a moment his features lost some of their harshness. 'There was no doubt my father died a happy man—for which I owe you a debt of gratitude.' His eyes became dark, like the deepest grey of a storm-tossed sea. 'However, I fail to comprehend why a beautiful young girl would be content with a man three times her age.'

Lisette could have offered an explanation, elaborated with facts, but instead she said slowly, 'I cared for him.' Jake's demons were his to slay, and she didn't feel inclined to help him.

His fingers tightened over her shoulders until she feared he must bruise the bones, and she gasped in pain.

'You knew him only a few months before you married him,' Jake threw ruthlessly, and she shook her head.

'You don't understand.'

'You're damned right I don't understand!'

She was unable to explain and unwilling to qualify the precise reason for her marriage. 'What Adam and I shared was special,' she said at last, and *felt* the silent force of Jake's anger.

'So special you can forget it every time I come within touching distance of you?' he demanded.

Stricken, she attempted to wrench herself out of his grasp.

'Oh, no, you don't,' Jake refused heavily. 'This time you're not running away.'

Anger rose to the surface, replacing any attempt at cool dignity. 'You can't make me stay,' she asserted.

'No?'

'Short of kidnapping, or sheer brute force,' Lisette retaliated, hating him. She wanted to hit back, to rage against his sheer purposeful intent.

It didn't help that she also wanted, *needed* him with an intensity that was positively frightening.

'Will you deny the degree of sexual chemistry we seem to generate?'

Her only protection was chilling anger, and she used it mercilessly. 'I don't regard that as a valid reason to go willingly into your bed.'

His eyes narrowed, assuming speculative calculation. 'What if I offered sufficient enticement?' he queried with silky detachment. 'Name your preference, Lisette. Jewellery, or cash?'

She was so cold, she could have sworn the blood in her veins had been replaced with ice.

'I'm not for sale.' Was that her voice? It sounded remote and distant, almost as if it belonged to someone else.

His eyes speared hers for what seemed an age. 'Everyone has their own price,' he said hatefully. 'Even you.'

She was breaking up inside, fragmenting into a thousand pieces. If he stayed another minute she'd say or do something regrettable. 'I'd like you to leave.'

For seemingly endless moments he just looked at her, and she was unable to gain anything from his expression. Then he reached out and caught hold of her shoulders, impelling her forward as his head lowered down to hers, and his hands slid down the length of her back as he imprisoned her close against him.

His mouth took possession of hers, hard and vaguely cruel in a demanding assault that brought a silent groan of despair. Slowly, and with deliberate intent, he began a wreaking devastation, his

tongue and his teeth destructive instruments that
alternately bruised and grazed the delicate inner
tissues.

She wanted to cry out against him, except no
sound would emerge, and he dispensed with her
struggles to be free of him with galling ease.

It was almost as if he sought to annihilate her
soul, and deep inside Lisette began to weep, hating
his sheer strength, his indomitable will.

Maybe he sensed her distress, for she became
aware of a subtle change in his mood, and the
mouth that had ravaged hers gentled slightly and
took on a teasing quality. The arms that bound her
to him loosened fractionally, and she felt his hands
roam across the contours of her back, then caress
the soft roundness of her bottom as he moulded
her against him.

Her mouth felt numb, the inner tissues swollen
and tender, and she gulped compulsively as he
began a light, teasing exploration with his tongue
in a gesture of expiation.

She wrenched her mouth away, then gave a
startled gasp as he trailed a path down the sensitive
cord of her neck to bury his lips in the vulnerable
hollow at its base.

'Don't,' Lisette groaned in a deep, impassioned
plea as one hand slid up to her nape, shaping it as
he threaded his fingers through her hair, then he
covered her lips with his own, caressing, teasing,
until she cried out against the spiralling sensation
that began somewhere deep inside and radiated
throughout her entire body.

His hand slid to her breast, and she gave a faint
moan of entreaty as his fingers began a delicate

tracing movement, enticing the soft bud into a peaking arousal so acute that she was conscious of its aching fullness.

Then she did cry out as his fingers reached for the zip fastener and slid it down so that her dress fell to the carpet at her feet, and even as she sought to cover her breasts he caught hold of her wrists and drew them apart.

Lisette struggled fruitlessly in an effort to free her arms. 'I hate what you're doing to me,' she cried in a tortured whisper, and he smiled—the faint curving slope of his mouth exhibiting a wealth of seduction.

'Poor *petite*,' he chided with gentle mockery. 'So emotionally wrought, when I've hardly even begun.'

She looked at him, seeing his strength, the degree of his resolve, and she was unable to suppress the involuntary shiver that shook her slim frame.

'Let me go.' She was beyond caring that the whispered plea almost amounted to begging.

He didn't answer, and instead his lips sought a deliberate trailing path from the edge of her neck along her collarbone to the curve of her shoulder, then back again, and she gasped out loud as his head inched lower towards the soft curve of her breast.

With incredible gentleness he kissed the delicate, burgeoning peak, opening his mouth to trace the aureole with his tongue before beginning an exquisite suckling that sent shards of sensation shooting along every nerve-fibre until she felt positively aflame with a desire so intense that it defied any definitive description.

Not content, he used his teeth to render an erotic tasting that placed her on a knife-edge between pleasure and pain, and just when she thought she could stand it no longer he shifted his attention to bestow a similar attention to its twin.

This was nothing less than madness, and she instinctively reached for his head, her fingers tangling restlessly with the dark thickness of his hair in an attempt to get him to stop.

She knew she should verbally entreat him to abandon a seduction so intensely erotic that if it were to continue there could be only one conclusion. Very soon she wouldn't possess the willpower to refuse, and while one part of her wanted the total satiation of the senses his possession would bring, the other part screamed out in silent rejection.

Perhaps Jake sensed her inner withdrawal, for she uttered a soundless gasp as he placed an arm beneath her knees and swept her close against his chest.

There could be no doubt as to his destination, and she began to struggle as he entered her bedroom. 'No. You can't,' she whispered as he lowered her down to the floor to stand within the firm circle of his arms.

He didn't answer for long, timeless seconds, then his head lowered down to hers and his mouth unerringly staked its claim in a plundering invasion that left her totally mindless.

Lisette had no conscious recollection of Jake discarding the remainder of her clothes, or his own. All she became aware of was the wildly seducing quality of his touch as he transported her high on

to an illusory, elusive plateau from which she never
wanted to descend.

At some stage Lisette became aware of sheets beneath her back, and light reflected from the bedside
lamp. His mouth, his hands were erotic instruments that knew no bounds as they conducted a
shameless exploration, taking impossible liberties
that she found vaguely shocking. Yet there was a
feeling of exultation, a sensual enjoyment she was
powerless to suppress, and she became totally enmeshed in a satiation of the senses.

His expertise was such that she had no conscious
knowledge of the tiny guttural cries she uttered in
acknowledgement of her pleasure, or the instinctive movements of her body as it increasingly
craved the fulfilment of his total possession.

She felt like a wanton, a wild, untamed being
that had emerged from deep within to accept a
conquering mastery so infinite, so incredibly erotic
that she thought she might faint from the force of
the swelling emotional tide.

There was a moment of brief discomfort as the
power of his initial thrust stretched silken tissues,
but she was beyond caring as she became caught
up in something so tumultuous, so achingly exquisite that it robbed her almost of the ability to
breathe.

Her body arched of its own volition, consciously
seeking the slow, measured pacing that she instinctively met and matched with an increasing hunger
as he led her towards the peak of sensual fulfilment.

An exquisite melting sensation consumed her
body as she drifted slowly into the aftermath of

passion. There was only now, and the delicious hazy glow that enveloped every one of her senses.

Gradually the reality of what she'd just shared, what she'd allowed to happen began to pervade her senses, and her eyes assumed a stark expression as soft colour suffused her cheeks.

Jake's arms held her imprisoned against him, and she stiffened slightly as she used her hands to push against his chest.

'Oh, no, *petite*,' he husked close to her ear. 'I won't permit you to cut and run.'

Where could she go? This was her apartment. 'Please.' She felt dangerously close to tears, and while she longed for the sanctuary of his embrace there was no way she could stay.

A strong hand captured first one wrist, then the other, and held them together, then he slid a hand beneath the heavy curtain of her hair and pulled her head into the curve of his shoulder.

Lisette felt his lips brush through her hair, then move to settle against her temple. He shifted slightly, curving her closer to the length of his body, and his mouth began a slow path of discovery as it trailed her forehead, brushing against each closed eyelid in turn before tracing the slope of her nose, the soft, bruised mouth that trembled beneath his touch.

'Please, Jake,' she begged breathlessly, and heard his soft, husky laugh.

'Go, little rabbit,' he teased. 'Just come back soon, hmm?'

Sliding out from the bed, she forced herself to walk slowly towards the large en suite bathroom, and she closed the door carefully behind her before crossing to the shower. The warm jet of water acted like a soft, pulsing balm to her sensitised skin, and she picked up the soap, beginning a cleansing process so incredibly thorough that her skin glowed from her ministrations.

A slight sound alerted her attention, and her mouth opened in a soundless gasp as the glass door slid open and Jake stepped calmly into the cubicle.

He filled her vision, so tall and splendidly built, his muscular frame a visual attestation to a daily fitness regime. Her eyes swept up to meet his incredibly dark, slumberous gaze, then her lashes lowered to form a protective veil against his blatant sensuality.

'I've finished,' she said in a voice choked with suppressed emotion as she endeavoured to move past him.

Without a word he picked up the soap and placed it in her hand, then, enclosing her hand within his own, he began slow circular movements over his chest.

His eyes never left hers, and after those first heart-stopping seconds she attempted to pull her hand free, only to have him tighten his grip.

What followed was an erotic experience, one that left her weak-willed and totally malleable, so that when he turned off the water it was all too easy to stand quiescent beneath his touch as he caught up a towel and slowly blotted the moisture from her body.

Wrapping the towel round his hips, he selected a bottle of scented body lotion from a collection of toiletries on top of the vanity unit and began smoothing it over her skin.

What ensued became a gentle, evocative massage that aroused every sensitive nerve-ending to fever-pitch, and Lisette couldn't have looked at him if her life had depended on it. She felt incredibly *alive*, aware of her body and the full potential of its sensuality in a way that she'd never imagined possible.

By the time he recapped the bottle she doubted her ability to stand. She was boneless, her limbs unable to support her slight stature, and she wasn't capable of voicing any protest when he swung her into his arms and carried her back to bed.

Laying her gently on the sheets, he sank down beside her, then, supporting his weight on one arm, he leaned forward and touched his lips to the inside of her knee and began trailing a tantalising path down to her ankle. Slowly, and with infinite care, his lips traversed every inch of skin, nipping gently with his teeth in vulnerable hollows, then bequeathed teasing love-bites to the tender curves of her breast. When he reached the most intimate crevices she was unable to prevent the involuntary arching of her body in its unbidden quest for his invasion.

The tiny husky pleas that emerged from her throat couldn't belong to her, Lisette thought dazedly. Yet they did, and her hands moved in silent supplication against his shoulders, her nails digging into the hard, sinewy muscle as she urged him to end this exquisite agony.

This time there was no restraint as he initiated an onslaught that gave no quarter as he took her to the heights of ecstasy and beyond in a manner that branded her as his own. There was a wild savagery in his possession, almost as if he was intent on ensuring she would only ever remember *him*, his mastery, his sensual virtuosity.

When at last it was over, he rolled on to his side, carrying her with him, and he cradled her gently against his chest until her deep, ragged breathing slowed to a normal beat.

How long she slept she had no idea, but it was dark when she woke, and at first she was unable to assimilate the weight across her waist, until memory resurfaced, bringing with it a wealth of remorse and shame.

She lay still, her mind tortured by the vivid events of the past few hours. One thing was certain. She couldn't remain here. Not in her bed, or even this apartment. To have him wake in the early morning hours and make love to her all over again would be more than she could bear.

She needed time to assemble her chaotic thoughts into some sort of rational order, time to *think*. And she couldn't do that unless she was alone.

Quietly, with the utmost care, she gradually eased her way free of him, then she slowly inched towards the edge of the bed.

She was almost holding her breath as she pulled on underwear before extracting a fashionable tracksuit from the wardrobe. Then she trod softly into the spare bedroom, where she collected an overnight bag and threw in a change of clothes, a few necessary items, make-up and toiletries. High-heeled shoes, and a business suit to wear into the office. All that remained were her car keys and her shoulder-bag.

Minutes later she was riding the elevator down to the basement car park. A further twenty, and she was standing at Reception of an inner-city hotel signing the register.

Her room was the usual pleasantly furnished, stereotyped, functional suite, and on locking the door she entered the en suite and ran a bath.

There was complimentary essence, and she poured in the entire contents of the bottle before emerging into the bedroom, where she discarded her clothes and pulled on a wrap.

A glance at the digital clock showed it was almost three-thirty, and she groaned out loud at the thought that there were only four hours before she would have to rise and get ready for work.

A leisurely soak in the hot, scented water did much to ease the slight ache of unused muscles. It did nothing whatsoever for the ache in her heart.

Jake's forceful image rose up to taunt her, and she closed her eyes against the vivid memory of his lovemaking. Dear lord in heaven, what had she done? Worse, how was she ever going to be able to go to work and maintain a business relationship with him?

Yet she *had* to do so. The only other alternative was to resign, and even then she'd have to work out at least a week's notice.

Oh, it was no use, she decided as she released the plug and stepped out of the bath. Briskly she towelled herself dry, then slipped into bed.

She was so weary, mentally and physically, that she should have fallen asleep the instant her head touched the pillow. Instead, she lay staring at the ceiling until the early dawn hours, when she fell into a fitful doze from which she came sharply awake at the sound of her requested wake-up call.

CHAPTER TEN

BY MID-MORNING Lisette had become a nervous wreck. Every time her desk phone rang, she expected it to be Jake. The resultant tension created havoc with her ability to concentrate, and twice she had to re-check requested alterations to an existing contract.

This was ridiculous, she decided, and walked to the coffee dispensing machine in the hope that strong black coffee might help allay at least some of her inner fears and insecurities.

The insistent peal of the phone almost an hour later brought a familiar return of tension, and Lisette reached for the receiver.

'Mr Hollingsworth is here.'

Damn. Her eyes clouded, and her teeth began to worry the soft underside of her lip in an unconscious gesture of anxiety.

'Lisette? Will you see him?'

Ethically, she could hardly refuse. 'Yes, of course. Show him in.'

He seemed to fill the room, his dark-suited frame appearing vaguely forbidding as he closed the distance between them.

Her smile was professionally polite, her eyes cautious as she gestured towards a nearby chair. It was bad enough that she had to see him, but she would far prefer to have him sitting down than towering over her exuding a silent threatening force.

In a way it was a relief. For the past few hours she'd run the gamut of multitudinous emotions, constantly swinging from a mixture of resentment and rage to varying degrees of pain.

'The relevant documentation for the Toorak property is being prepared, and will be available soon,' she told him.

His hard, rough-chiselled features assembled into a uncompromising mask, and his appraisal was swift and hatefully analytical as he raked her slim form.

'That isn't why I'm here.'

Lisette momentarily closed her eyes in exasperation. 'You must be aware I can't indulge in personal matters during office hours.'

'*Personal matters*, Lisette?' His gleaming gaze openly mocked any attempt she made towards conventional formality.

Remembering how she'd lain in his arms, a willing supplicant to everything he chose to bestow, brought a soft tinge of colour to her cheeks. Quite deliberately she flicked a glance at the watch on her wrist, then arched a cool eyebrow as she returned his gaze. 'Must I remind you this is hardly the time or the place?'

Something glittered darkly in the depth of his eyes, and for a brief moment she felt afraid.

'Name a time and a place.'

'And if I choose not to?' She had to have taken leave of her senses, baiting him like this. Yet it was almost as if some devilish imp had invaded her brain.

'Then I will.'

It would be so easy to succumb, to accept what he offered without challenge. Except somehow it wasn't enough.

'I think it would be better if we don't see each other again,' she said.

Eyes as dark and as cold as polished onyx struck through to her heart with the precision of a rapier-sharp sabre.

'Did you use the same inflexible technique with my father?'

The shock of his words drained the blood from her face, and her eyes felt incredibly large as they ached with the painful threat of tears.

For what seemed an age she could only look at him, bereft of the power of speech, then with supreme effort she marshalled her resources and rose to her feet behind the desk. It took every ounce of resolve to walk towards the door with unhurried ease. She managed it—just, opening it quietly before turning towards him. 'If you'll excuse me, I really must get on with my work.'

'I need those papers within an hour.' His voice was hard, obdurate, and totally inflexible.

'You'll have them.' But I won't be here to give them to you, she decided silently.

Without a further word he walked past her, not in anger, but with calm, leisurely ease.

Quietly she closed the door behind him, leaning back against it as she closed her eyes. She felt totally numb, devoid of any emotion.

How long she stood there she had little idea, and it was only the seemingly loud jangle of the phone that brought her back to the present as she crossed to her desk to take the call. Five minutes, she determined as she checked her watch on replacing the receiver bare seconds later. They could have been five hours.

Collecting her briefcase, she caught up her shoulder-bag, then left her office and made her way towards the lift. Within minutes she was in the car, easing it up to street level, and once free of the city she simply drove, uncaring of anything except her need to put as much distance between her and the hateful man who'd swept into her life and turned it upside-down.

An hour later she pulled into a petrol station and placed two calls while the attendant filled the tank. First she rang Maman, who listened, and sagely kept her silence, adding only an insistence to keep in touch and take care.

Leith Andersen was not so understanding. However, he did reluctantly agree to grant her leave of absence when threatened with a verbal resignation.

Unwilling to return to her apartment, she booked into a hotel for the night, and the following morning she collected what clothes she needed, and boarded a flight north to a tropical island resort where sunshine and relaxation abounded. A place where it was possible to push Jake Hollingsworth to the far reaches of her mind.

*   *   *

The island was an idyllic retreat, a popular tourist resort specialising in total relaxation, where the guests were offered a variety of sports activities, with the choice to participate left entirely to the individual.

Lisette rose early each morning, slipping a beach-jacket over her bikini to embark on a leisurely walk along the sandy foreshore. Sometimes she swam in the cool, clear sea, or chose to stroke several lengths of the pool before returning to her unit for breakfast. The remainder of the day was usually spent enjoying the warm sunshine while browsing through a magazine or reading a book. In the evenings she ordered by room service, preferring her own company to joining the island's holiday-makers in the restaurant.

Each day saw the arrival and departure of a few guests—by launch, or helicopter. Lisette became accustomed to the varying sounds, and rarely took time to lift her head from her book to view the incoming visitors.

The swift-turning rotor-blades whining to a slow halt a week after Lisette's arrival hardly warranted her attention. Yet for some inexplicable reason she experienced a vague sense of apprehension, and despite the tropical sunshine a faint chill shivered across the surface of her skin, raising all her fine body hairs in a gesture of self-protection.

Imagination, she chided silently, returning her attention to the printed page. Except that the words no longer held any appeal, and after several minutes she simply rested her head down on to her arms and closed her eyes. The sun had a soporific effect,

lulling her into a state of inertia, and she lapsed
into a light doze.

Quite what disturbed her, she wasn't sure. It was
almost as if an elusive sixth sense was intent on
playing havoc with her equilibrium.

Unsettled, she closed her book and rose to her
feet. The afternoon sun would soon lose its warmth
anyway, and besides, a little exercise would help
ease the slight tenseness in her muscles.

Removing her sunglasses, she placed them on top
of her book and took the few steps necessary to
bring her to the pool's edge. Executing a neat, clean
dive into the sparkling blue water, she resurfaced
and stroked a few leisurely laps before pausing at
the pool's tiled edge to lever herself on to the wide
ledge. Water streamed off her body, and her hands
went automatically to her hair to squeeze out the
excess moisture.

'Towel?'

Lisette froze at the sound of that slightly accented drawl. In what seemed like slow motion she
turned to have her worst fears confirmed as Jake's
forceful frame filled her vision.

Looming impossibly tall, he portrayed restrained
power—like a panther controlled by a leash, and
none the less dangerous simply because of the
restriction.

Lisette's eyes flew to his, becoming trapped in
their darkness as several chaotic thoughts fought
for supremacy, the foremost of which had to be
how he'd managed to determine her whereabouts.

'Your mother,' Jake revealed quietly, watching the expressive play of emotions chase fleetingly across her features.

'Maman? She would n-never——' Lisette faltered to a halt as he reached down and caught hold of her hand, pulling her to stand beside him.

'I managed to convince her it was essential I find you.'

'Indeed?' Dark golden-green eyes gleamed with latent anger, clashing violently with the daunting steel evident in his as he wrapped the towel round her slim curves. His fingers brushed the curve of her breast and she reacted as if touched by flame.

'Your presence on this island is an impossible intrusion,' she bit out in a furious undertone, and became further incensed as his lips curved to form a cynical smile.

'Shall we conduct this conversation in your unit or mine?'

'We have nothing to discuss.'

Without a word he placed an arm beneath her knees and swept her high against his chest. Ignoring her startled gasp, he carried her with effortless ease, oblivious to the curious, speculative glances his action generated.

'Put me down!' she demanded, furious almost beyond words, and she nearly died at the smouldering intensity evident in his gaze.

'You're so small—a featherweight,' he voiced with a degree of repressed violence. 'It scares me almost to death.'

The breath caught in her throat, momentarily rendering her speechless. 'Jake——'

'We're nearly there.'

She was supremely conscious of the broadness of his shoulders beneath her hands, and her stomach gave a painful lurch as he ascended the few steps necessary to bring him to the door of his unit.

Shifting her weight slightly, he retrieved a key from his pocket and inserted it into the lock, then he walked inside and closed the door.

'Put me *down*!' Lisette cried.

Without a word he released her to stand within the circle of his arms, and when she made to break free of him he merely tightened his hold.

'Damn you,' she condemned, hating him for a variety of reasons too numerous to mention. 'Haven't you done enough?'

He searched her features, taking in the angry bleakness in those splendid hazel eyes, the slight tinge of pink colouring the contours of her cheekbones, the proud tilt of her chin.

Something flared in his eyes, an infinitesimal flame that subsided to re-emerge as wry humour as he lifted a hand and touched a finger to her cheek.

Her lips parted slightly to frame the words condemning him to hell, except that they never emerged. Instead, she stood in icy silence, her eyes warring openly with his.

'Why, Lisette?' His eyes appeared so deep that she couldn't even begin to define their depths. 'Why keep from me the fact that treatment and medication had rendered Adam impotent?' Jake queried after what seemed an age.

No conventional niceties. Just a direct aim for the jugular! She stood perfectly still, locked into immobility, and her voice caught in her throat, temporarily denying the power of speech.

'Did you think I wouldn't find out?' he persisted.

He was all tautly controlled power, his impact so strong, so darkly magnificent that she felt almost afraid.

'Amazing how I could have been so blind,' he drawled with a degree of self-derision. 'There had always been a logical explanation for your marriage to Adam, yet I failed to see one.'

She was aware of an elemental quality, a self-imposed restraint that tripped her pulse and sent it racing out of control.

'Do you have any conception *why*?' he demanded with dangerous softness.

Her eyes became enmeshed with his, and there wasn't a single thing she could think of to say.

'Three years ago I flew in to this country to witness my father's second marriage—to a girl young enough to be his granddaughter.' His eyes darkened and assumed an immeasurable bleakness. 'I took one look at you, and knew it should have been me standing there beside you, *me* who had the right to share your bed.'

She opened her mouth, but no sound emerged, and she closed it again. A haunting vulnerability clouded her eyes, and she lowered her lashes in a gesture of protective self-defence.

'The knowledge rocked the very ground from beneath my feet,' Jake declared wryly. 'I was a self-confessed cynic who didn't believe anything other than passion prompted by sexual desire could happen in the reality of life.'

Lisette felt as if she was teetering on the edge of a precipice, and she looked at him carefully, seeing the latent fire in the depths of his eyes, as well as something she dared not attempt to define.

'I did the only thing possible. I walked away.' He lifted a hand and brushed gentle fingers down the length of her cheek. 'To salve my conscience, I allowed myself to believe you'd set my father's considerable wealth in your sights and used feminine wiles to charm him all the way to the altar.'

Jake paused, then continued quietly, 'Afterwards I had to come to terms with the fact that Adam had chosen not to reveal the true state of his health to anyone other than you. It hurt me deeply that I didn't have the opportunity to spend time with him, to say all the things I wanted him to know. Words he deserved to hear.'

Lisette swallowed the lump that had risen in her throat, and her voice emerged as choked and husky. 'He was an exceptional man.' She wanted to reach out and offer Jake a measure of solace, yet she didn't quite have the courage.

'For more than a year I threw myself into ensuring Hollingsworth International achieved accolades in the business sector. It wasn't enough.' A slight smile twisted the edges of his mouth, but there was no cynicism, no mockery apparent. 'No matter how hard I tried, I was unable to get you out of my mind.'

Her heart stopped, then picked up on an increased beat, and for several long seconds her voice seemed locked into an agonising silence.

He traced an idle finger down the smooth column of her throat, his smile faintly wry as she reared back from his touch. 'Afraid, Lisette?'

Her eyes remained steady, despite the increased tempo of her pulse. 'I don't fear you.'

'Perhaps you should.' He appeared fascinated by the rapid beating in the hollow at the base of her throat, and she cursed her body's tell-tale reaction to his potent brand of sexual chemistry. 'At least be grateful for the time it took me to discover your whereabouts.' His eyes speared hers, dark and obsidian with latent emotion, and she stood perfectly still as his hand curved round her throat, then slid to cup her chin. 'Had you been in Melbourne, I would probably have strangled you.'

'If you had,' she uttered a trifle fiercely, 'I would have charged you with assault.'

His fingers slid to her nape and curled into the damp length of her hair as he shaped and tilted her head. 'I'd never have allowed you to reach the phone. Afterwards, you wouldn't have had sufficient energy to move.' His mouth moved gradually lower to pause within an inch of hers. 'Then I would have taken you again, slowly and with such infinite eroticism that there could be no room for doubt...' he paused again fractionally as he gathered her close against him '... as to whom you belong, or why.'

'Sex on its own isn't a good enough reason for anything,' she denied, desperately attempting to twist her mouth away from his impending possession.

'Just what is it you imagine I have in mind?'

I don't know, an inner voice cried out. But it can't be what I want. Fairy-tales rarely come true, and dreams are merely false illusions.

Her gaze didn't falter, although it took considerable effort to keep the hurt from her voice. 'Maman had no right to tell you——'

'Your mother is incredibly loyal,' he intervened with a tinge of cynicism. 'It took considerable persuasion to convince her to reveal your whereabouts.'

'I still don't understand——'

His eyes gleamed with a degree of self-mockery. 'She relented on hearing she'll have me as her son-in-law in the very near future.'

Lisette froze, her eyes dilating with shock. 'That was unforgivable.'

Jake smiled, his mouth curving gently as he brushed his lips across her own. 'It's the truth. I want my ring on your finger. *You* in my bed all night long. The security of official sanction in the form of a marriage certificate.' His smile broadened as his eyes captured each fleeting movement of her beautiful features. 'Not merely as a link to legality, but as proof of a lifetime commitment.' He touched gentle fingers to the softness of her mouth. 'I love your fierce, defensive pride, the sweetness that comes from the heart—everything that is *you*.'

He caught hold of her left hand, then with care he gently slid off the slim diamond-encrusted band and replaced it on the third finger of her right hand. 'This is where it belongs,' he said softly. 'A reminder of Adam, and the part I believe he played in bringing us together.'

He lowered his head and kissed her, slowly and with such infinite sweetness that she had to blink quickly against the sudden threat of tears. Then his arms moulded her close as his mouth closed over her own in a kiss that was undeniably possessive.

If he could have absorbed her, body and soul, he would have done so, and Lisette became a willing supplicant, matching his ardour with her own.

When at last he lifted his head she could only look at him in total bemusement, and he smiled at the bruised softness of her mouth before bending low to brush his lips across her own. In an unbidden gesture she lifted a hand and touched her fingers to his cheek, her eyes wide and luminous as he buried his mouth into the softness of her palm.

'I'm tempted to beat you for remaining silent on an issue which could have saved me a lot of personal anguish,' he murmured.

Her eyes sought his, silently beseeching his compassion. 'You have to understand that I would never have married Adam if the circumstances had been other than they were,' she offered a trifle shakily. 'We slept in separate rooms until the last few weeks, when I insisted on being close enough to hear him if he should call out in the night. Even so, there was a qualified nurse in residence. He had the very best of care,' she relayed gently.

For a brief instant his eyes assumed a tinge of cynicism. 'I would have done better to have trusted my father's judgement and been more intuitive to his state of health—aware that human need was a logical reason for a marriage I refused to condone.' His eyes never left hers, and Lisette almost died at

the depth of emotion she saw there. Her own
pricked with aching tears that welled then spilled
over to run slowly in twin rivulets down each cheek.

'Don't cry,' Jake groaned huskily, tracing the
path of her tears with the soft pad of his thumb.

'I'm not,' Lisette denied shakily, all too aware
that Adam would have approved—probably even
hoped for this very outcome between his only son
and the girl he'd regarded with so much affection.

'This is for you,' Jake said gently, reaching into
the pocket of his jacket, then slipping a large
diamond solitaire ring on to her finger. 'With all
my love.'

'I haven't said I'll marry you.' The words slipped
out without much thought, and she almost cried
out loud at the sudden bleakness that darkened his
eyes.

'You want me to beg?'

She went curiously still, locked into silence for a
few seconds at the enormity of holding so much
power. 'Would you?'

A small, faintly cynical smile twisted his lips.
'Oh, yes. Does that admission frighten you?' His
eyes became faintly hooded. 'I warn that it should.
Where you are concerned, I feel so incredibly
humble I can't find the words to offer an adequate
explanation.'

A strange lightness lifted her heart, and a bewitching sparkle lit her eyes. 'Perhaps you could
try.'

A gleam warmed the darkness of his steely gaze,
and his mouth parted in a gesture of musing self-

mockery. 'Minx,' he derided in husky admonition. 'I'd much prefer a practical demonstration.'

'Jake——' She faltered to a halt, torn between wanting him and the need to remove every last vestige of her own insecurity.

His smile was incredibly gentle, his eyes so dark and warm that her mouth trembled slightly of its own volition. His hands slid up her shoulders to cup her face, and she almost died at the wealth of passion evident in his expression. 'I need to love you. To wipe out all the hurt and the pain. To show you exactly what you mean to me. The pivotal core of my existence.'

Her whole body was on fire, consumed by a desire so intense that it took every ounce of will-power to breathe evenly. Slowly she reached up and clasped her hands at his nape, then she stood on the tips of her toes and gently pulled his head down to hers. Hesitantly she grazed his lips with her own, her touch tentative and unsure, and she gave a soundless gasp as his tongue edged out to tease hers, stroking tantalising light brushstrokes in an evocative, sensual exploration that became the initial orchestration of something so infinite, so devastating that she began to wonder if she could survive with her emotions intact.

The silken scraps of her bikini fell to the carpeted floor, joined within minutes by his shirt and trousers.

She hesitated as her fingers poised at the band of his briefs. Her lips trembled slightly as she touched him, her eyes widening as she felt the immediate surge of power.

'Don't stop,' he groaned. Two simple words, voiced with such husky emotion that it was impossible not to be aware of the precariousness of his control.

Yet he was holding back, letting her set the pace, and for the first time Lisette tasted the feeling of power a woman could have over a man, exultant for a few brief seconds before letting her hands drift slowly up to link together at his nape.

'You're so much better at this than I am.'

His eyes darkened measurably, and his faint smile was self-derisory. 'I feel like a schoolboy. Tentative, and incredibly afraid of hurting you.'

Tentative? *Jake*? She didn't want or covet that brand of power. 'You couldn't hurt me,' she said simply, knowing it to be the truth.

'Yet I did,' he owned with deep regret. 'Out of anger, and blind, jealous rage. Against my father, who saw the sweetness of your soul and made it his. Against myself, for not seeing you first. And you, because you didn't conform to any role in which I cast you.'

Reaching up, she brushed his mouth with her own, parting her lips in invitation of an evocative possession he didn't hesitate to provide, and just when she thought the kissing would never end he eased his mouth away and began a slow, trailing descent to her breast to take his fill before tracing a path low over the indentation of her navel.

From there he moved steadily downward, kneeling at her feet as the tasting assumed such exquisite torture that she cried out, curling her fingers into his hair in an agony of agitation, her body unconsciously arching to accommodate his seeking erotic touch, and unaware that his hands had moved to support the base of her spine.

She was vaguely aware of begging, small, guttural, sobbing sounds torn from the depths of her being, and just when she thought she could bear no more he began a slow upward path to suckle shamelessly at her breasts, then his mouth travelled to close over hers with such devastation that she burned, going up in flames in a total conflagration of the senses.

She'd had no sensation of being carried, she decided vaguely as he sank down on to the bed, gently positioning her slim frame over his.

With exquisite care he accommodated her to accept his length, witnessing her faint surprise with a warm, indolent smile as he urged her head down to his, and she exulted in his kiss, loving the feel of him inside her as he began to move—gently at first, then with a quiet urgency that fuelled her own fire to such an unbearable degree that she actually held on to him, afraid to let go in case she might fall.

Then the feeling began to ebb, decreasing its intensity to a delicious warm ache which she instinctively knew would need little urging to flare into glorious life all over again.

Like an ecstatic, mischievous kitten needing to test its provocativeness, she stretched, her expression one of total self-satisfaction as she met his dark, slightly hooded gaze.

'Is this likely to happen very often?' Lisette queried lightly, loving the tantalising touch of his fingers as he trailed them in an explorative caress over the softness of her skin.

'The climactic orgasmic explosion, or just sex?'

The thought of describing what they'd just shared as 'sex' seemed a contradiction in terms, for it was more than that—so much more.

'I prefer lovemaking.' For two people so totally in accord with each other the physical consummation was an extension of the mind, transcending mere pleasure.

'So do I,' Jake vowed gently, as he rolled her over to lie beneath him. 'And yes—often.'

Her eyes assumed a soft, faintly wicked gleam. 'I think I could get used to it,' she teased, and the soft, husky laugh barely found voice as his mouth closed over hers in passionate possession.

CHAPTER ELEVEN

THEY were married two days later. A whispery grey day with intermittent glimpses of sunshine in between light squally showers.

Lisette didn't care if the rain fell in an unabating deluge. She was so happy. It glowed from within, lighting her eyes and curving her lips into a bewitching smile.

The long, slim-fitting wedding-gown in pale cream silk hugged her slender figure, its demurely styled neckline and long fitted sleeves highlighted by a full-length finely-embroidered veil.

She looked infinitely fragile as she joined the tall, dark, formally-suited man at the altar, and together they solemnly exchanged their vows, totally oblivious to the presence of anyone else.

Afterwards, they sipped champagne, forked a few morsels from each course, then slowly circled the small cluster of guests, their hands entwined as they indulged in polite small talk.

Frequently their eyes would meet and cling, their message unmistakable, and more than a few present felt a clutch of envy for the wealth of restrained emotion evident.

Eventually, in pairs, and singly, everyone began to depart. Louise was the last to leave, and her quick hug and brilliant smile hid a tinge of wistful bemusement as she farewelled her daughter, then al-

lowed her son-in-law the pleasure of formall
escorting her to a waiting car.

'Take good care of her,' she begged quietly as h
bent to brush his lips to her cheek.

'For the rest of my life,' he promised softly, the
he closed the car door, waiting until the drive
pulled away before moving back into the house.

The caterers had been efficient, and apart fror
a few partly filled ashtrays, a half-dozen glasses
there was little evidence to witness that a weddin
and reception had taken place in the beautifull
furnished lounge.

The process of locking up took only a fe
minutes. A soft sound of chinking crystal cam
from the direction of the kitchen, and he move
towards it with leisurely strides, his hands autc
matically lifting to loosen his tie, then unfasten th
uppermost button at the neck of his shirt.

Lisette turned slightly, sensing his approach, an
her mouth parted into a bewitching, faintl
winsome smile.

This was the first night in their new home. A
home for which Jake had utilised an army c
tradespeople and a vaguely shocking amount c
money to ensure that the redecoration necessary wa
complete in time to host their wedding reception

He came to stand behind her, sliding his arm
round her waist as he buried his lips against th
soft curve of her nape. 'I've been waiting to do thi
for the past few hours,' he murmured, teasing th
scented hollow with his tongue.

A faint bubble of laughter emerged from he
throat in husky humour. 'Really?'

His teeth nipped the sensitive edge of her neck in silent admonition. 'As a prelude to total ravishment.' His mouth opened over the sensitised flesh, playing an erotic, evocative game that succeeded in sending shivers of anticipation arrowing through her body.

'That sounds promising,' she teased, gasping faintly as he turned her and swung her into his arms. She lifted her hands and linked them behind his head, exulting in the hard, measured beat of his heart as he reached the stairs and began to ascend the thick-carpeted treads, carrying her with ease.

In the large airy bedroom at the end of the wide hallway he lowered her gently to her feet.

'Happy?'

There was something in his voice Lisette couldn't quite pin-point, a faint, almost imperceptible hesitancy that was totally alien. His eyes were dark, almost black with deep, brooding passion, and she looked at him with wide-eyed solemnity as he lifted a hand and let his fingers trail across her cheek.

'Do you need to ask?'

The edge of his mouth twisted fractionally, and for a brief second he looked strangely vulnerable. Then the fleeting expression was gone, and she wondered if she'd imagined it.

He knew. He had to. During the past few days she'd given everything of herself, responding with uninhibited delight, an eager, generous pupil beneath his sensual expertise. Yet each time she'd drawn back from voicing the words. So clear, so meaningful, yet so elusive. Afterwards she'd lain

in his arms, dreamily exhausted with complete
satiation before drifting into sleep.

'I love you.' Her voice trembled slightly, and she
swallowed in an attempt to clear the faint lump that
seemed to have risen in her throat.

His eyes darkened, then became liquid with suppressed emotion. 'I began to wonder if you were
ever going to tell me.'

'I thought you must already know.'

'Where you're concerned, I'm incredibly
defenceless.'

She lifted a hand and let her fingers roam over
the strongly etched bones of his face before coming
to rest at his mouth. 'Dearest Jake. You're the other
half of my soul.' Her lips parted in a winsome smile.
'My love, my life.'

He closed his eyes, then slowly opened them, and
she almost drowned in their brilliance. 'Show me.'

She did. With great care, and all the love there
was to give. Something she knew would be theirs
for a lifetime.

PRESENTS® *plus*

Meet Griff Morgan, a man on the rebound, and Sarah
Williams, a woman who *already* has a broken heart.

And then there's Sam Hardy, who simply loves 'em and leaves
'em, and Lauren Bell, who's still haunted by *one* man from
her past.

These are just some of the passionate men and women you'll
discover each month in Harlequin Presents Plus—two longer
and dramatic new romances by some of the best-loved authors
writing for Harlequin Presents. Share their exciting stories—
their heartaches and triumphs—as each falls in love.

Don't miss
THE JILTED BRIDEGROOM by Carole Mortimer
Harlequin Presents Plus #1559
and
SLEEPING PARTNERS by Charlotte Lamb
Harlequin Presents Plus #1560

Harlequin Presents Plus

The best has just gotten better!
Available in June wherever Harlequin books are sold.

Fifty red-blooded, white-hot, true-blue hunks from every
State in the Union!

Beginning in May, look for MEN MADE IN AMERICA!
Written by some of our most popular authors, these
stories feature fifty of the strongest, sexiest men, each
from a different state in the union!

Two titles available every other month at your favorite
retail outlet.

In July, look for:

CALL IT DESTINY by Jayne Ann Krentz (Arizona)
ANOTHER KIND OF LOVE by Mary Lynn Baxter
(Arkansas)

In September, look for:

DECEPTIONS by Annette Broadrick (California)
STORMWALKER by Dallas Schulze (Colorado)

You won't be able to resist MEN MADE IN AMERICA!